Who Do I Run To Now?

Who Do I Run To Now?

Anna Black

www.urbanbooks.net

Urban Books, LLC
300 Farmingdale Road, N.Y.-Route 109
Farmingdale, NY 11735

ISBN 13: 978-1-64556-447-8
ISBN 10: 1-64556-447-9

First Trade Paperback Printing February 2023
Printed in the United States of America

10 9 8 7 6 5 4 3 2 1

Distributed by Kensington Publishing Corp.
Submit Orders to:
Customer Service
400 Hahn Road
Westminster, MD 21157-4627
Phone: 1-800-733-3000
Fax: 1-800-659-2436

Who Do I Run To Now?

Anna Black

Chapter One

Isaiah Lawton

He walked into the kitchen with the last box he had retrieved from his SUV to see Janiece tearing away paper from the glass dish she had in her hand. They were all moved into their new home, and he could not have been happier that day. Two years had zoomed by, and he was madly in love with his wife.

"Hey, you." Janiece noticed that he had entered the room.

"Hey, beautiful," he said, putting the box down. He hurried over to plant a soft kiss on Janiece's lips, and she gave him that smile he was always happy to see.

"Is that the last one?" she asked, nodding her head toward the box he had put down.

"Yes, that is it, and I can tell you that we will be here until we grow old and die. Moving fuckin' sucks," Isaiah said, looking around. They had a lot of work ahead of them, and he was certainly not up for it.

"Well, I spent my day separating and putting boxes in the right room, so it's a bit organized, at least. Doesn't resemble yesterday after the movers left."

"No, it's not as horrible as yesterday, but we still got a lot of unpacking," he added.

"True indeed, so go grab a drink and put on some good music, because it's time to work, baby," she ordered.

"I know we got a lot to tackle, but yo' man thinks we should take a little break. We've been moving for the last couple of days, and I'd like you to go upstairs and bust open one of your wardrobe boxes to find a sexy dress to wear, and we shower, dress, and go out for a nice dinner. These boxes and shit can wait. We need a decent meal, baby," he suggested.

"Babe, no, you know we need to tackle this house. Besides, going through boxes to find a dress, shoes, perfume, and even my makeup sounds exhausting. We can order in, make cocktails, blast our favorite music, and tackle all of these damn boxes," she countered.

"Come on, baby," he insisted as he walked over to her. He then embraced her from behind, pulling her in as close as possible. He planted a gentle kiss on her ear and then continued to persuade her. "Jai, baby, you are not going to deny me tonight. You know you can come up with something fabulous. I wanna take you out. I don't want to order takeout. We've been doing that for the last month since we started packing, so please, baby, don't make me beg, because you know damn well I will," he said with hopes that she'd oblige.

"Fine, okay, okay, Isaiah, damn. I'll go up and find something to put on, and you'd better not complain about how long it takes me to get ready," she said, turning to him. The smile she wore was confirmation that she was just as welcoming of the break as he was. He gave her a quick kiss before allowing her to leave the kitchen. She headed for the steps, and he was two steps behind her. He followed her into their master and then into their walk-in closet. She went for a labeled dress box, and he watched her quickly open it. He pulled his shirt over his head and tossed it to the floor with a smile.

"Damn, I didn't know you'd come up in this closet and start undressing in front of me like that," she said.

"Oh, well, I only have a couple of boxes of clothes, so it won't take me forever to find something to wear, so I figured I'd shower while you figured it all out," he said, undoing his jeans.

"Again, you got me thinking about something other than food," she said, watching him remove his jeans.

"Well, we can take this moment to christen our closet and then dress for dinner," he said teasingly. It didn't take a lot of convincing. She immediately started to undress. Nipples were erect. A look of desire in her eyes for him gave him a stiff dick.

She moved closer to him. "That idea sounds really nice," she said before wrapping her arms around his neck. They kissed passionately as he moved his fingers to her core. He began to rub and play around in her center to get her tunnel super wet for his pleasurable thrusting. After a few moments of tongue and finger dancing, she pulled back. When she went into a squat, he knew what she was about to do, and he prayed that the day's events wouldn't cause her to pause. Not that he had done a lot of physical work other than the last six or seven boxes, but he hoped that he was still fresh enough for his wife to perform.

"Babe, you don't have to. I need to probably hit the shower," he suggested.

She kissed his head. "Baby, you're good," she said before wrapping her sexy-ass glossed lips around his steal pipe.

He liked it wet, and he liked her tongue movements, so he always had to watch. More blood rushed to his tool, and he hadn't made love to her in a while, since they'd moved, so he pulled away.

"Bae, what's wrong?"

"Nothing. You are all right and perfect, and I want to just be inside you when I release, that's all." He pulled her close and kissed her deeply. He was so aroused he sucked on her bottom lip and then her chin.

"I love kissing you, baby," she panted between kisses and breaths. "I'm ready to feel you, baby," she said and leaned back against the closet wall. He made it a point to kiss her face and suck on her nipples before her legs were around his waist. He planted his feet firmly as her back rested against the wall, and he easily slid in.

"Ahhhhhh," she moaned, and he froze. It hadn't been that long, but he wanted to bust as soon as he entered. "Give it to me," she purred, and he counted to ten and then went to work.

He pounded her body to ecstasy, and he was proud to give his woman an explosion that caused her thighs to tremble. The way her body responded to his had his soldiers ready, and he pumped harder and harder as he watched the way her titties bounced. He wanted to take one inside his mouth, but he was in no mood to catch one from bouncing at the beat of his thrust.

When he exploded, he had to keep all his strength to keep from dropping her lower half wrapped around him. On wobbly legs, he pulled out and let her down. "You are too much," he said.

"No, you are," she panted. She stayed leaning on the wall, and she looked around the closet. "You still want to go out?"

"Fuck, no! Shit, I need a shower and then a damn nap."

She approached him and placed her hands on his shoulders. "You can have both, but when you get up, we are unpacking these damn boxes," she confirmed and then walked out of the closet.

"Okay," he agreed as he headed to their master bath. He went to relieve his bladder, and she walked in and started the shower. She stepped into the shower, and he joined her.

"Hey, what are you doing in my shower?" she teased.

"I can't shower with my wife?" he asked, embracing her from behind.

"Yes, Mr. Lawton, you can." She smiled, and he kissed her neck.

"You make me so happy," he said.

"Do I?

"Yes, and the last two years have been bumpy with me leaving to finish up in Killeen. So many times, I thought . . ." He paused.

She turned to him. "Thought what?"

He shook his head. "Never mind. The point is we are together and happy. This house will be filled with so much love and joy."

She smiled and nodded a little, agreeing with him. After a quick kiss, they lathered each other, and after playing around a little longer, they got out and put on some loungewear. Isaiah did not take a nap, ordered Chinese, and they got to work on the boxes.

Chapter Two

Kerry Paxton

"Sweet home Chicago," K.P. said when he pulled into Kimberly's circular driveway. He was in the process of moving back to the Windy City. His company had done so well that he was now opening a second branch in Chicago, so he was excited. He liked Las Vegas, but it was just hard with the kids being so far away from their mom. Things were finally amicable, and they were doing better than ever.

She had married her lover, Rodney, after he basically rescued her from going to prison for her assault on his ex's sister. Kimberly spent less than nine months in jail because of the money and the power of her father's and Rodney's connections. It took them less than a year to get her out. She got off with a slap on the wrist and was now on parole. Initially, her father turned his back on her due to the embarrassment of Kimberly's actions, but he didn't let her suffer too long. Although both of Kimberly's parents saw it fit for K.P. to have full custody of their kids, they begged him to still allow Kimberly to have visitation. K.P. wanted to say absolutely not, but his children loved and adored their mother, so he agreed. He was sure that Kimberly would never harm them, so he was okay with Kimberly being a part of their lives.

"Kayla, baby, wake up. We're here," K.P. said, shaking her a bit.

K.J. was in the back seat sleeping too because it was after eleven p.m. Before he could undo his seat belt, Kimberly opened the passenger-side door. He knew she was anxious to see them because they hadn't been home since their last spring break. K.P. waited for the school year to end before he made their move.

"Kayla, sweetie, wake up," Kimberly said, kissing her face. "Hey, Kerry," she said, acknowledging him.

"Hey," he replied and got out to get his son from the back seat.

"Ed, our houseman, will come out for their things," she said.

"Okay," K.P. replied and then shook K.J. to wake him. "Are you coming in?"

He needed to use her bathroom, so he answered, "Yes."

Kimberly smiled with a slight nod, and she and Kayla headed up the walkway. K.P. walked in with K.J., and then Kimberly pulled him into a tight hug.

"Oooh, Momma missed you so much. I have so many fun things planned for us this summer," she told them.

K.P. didn't want to take her attention from her reunion with the children, but he had to go to the bathroom. "Kim, which way is the bathroom?"

She gave a point and a couple of quick directions. K.P. went and admired the beautiful home she and Rodney lived in. He smiled because that was definitely the scale of the house that Kimberly always wanted, and after all the evil deeds she had done, she still landed on top. He washed and dried his hands, and Rodney was there when he returned to the foyer.

"Kerry, how are you?" Rodney asked with his right hand extended.

K.P. shook it. "Hey, Rodney, I'm cool. How are you, man?"

"I'm doing well," he replied.

"Great," he said and then turned to Kimberly. "I'm going to head out."

"Okay," she said, and he kissed the kids and said his goodbyes. He made his exit, and Kimberly called out his name before he could get to the end of the walkway. He paused in his tracks, hoping there wouldn't be any drama or she wouldn't say anything to piss him off.

"Yeah," he answered before turning in her direction.

"Thank you. We have a rocky past, and this was not easy for you, so thank you for allowing the summer with the kids. I missed them more than words," she expressed, and he believed her.

"Hey, no problem. They've been anxiously waiting for this time with you, so I hope you guys have a great summer."

"You know you are welcome to come by and see them anytime?"

"Yeah, I know, and this is a huge favor to me because I'll be back and forth between here and Vegas until the move is complete, so this works out for the both of us."

"Yes, I guess it does. Where are you staying while you're here? We have a million rooms here, so you are welcome."

"Kimberly, you know I'm not going to take you up on an offer to stay with you and your husband. Nah, I'm good."

"Yeah, that is kinda crazy, right?"

"Yes, it is. I'll be at Marcus's for a couple of weeks until I close on my house."

"That's cool. Too bad we sold the house in Lansing. You could've stayed there."

He shook his head. "No, too many bad memories. I'm glad it's sold."

"Yeah, you're right," she agreed.

They stood there silently for a moment, and K.P. noticed that she looked really good. Her hair was straightened, and her makeup was light and not piled on like back when she was his wife. Her sleeveless halter clung to her slender but curvy body, and she no longer resembled the crazy Kimberly he was married to. He wanted to compliment her, but he decided not to.

"Well, I'll be going now. Good night, Kim."

"Good night, K.P., and it was good seeing you."

He nodded, and then she turned to head back to the house. He got into the car, and when he jumped on the expressway, he fought the urge to take the exit that would lead him to Janiece's condo. He thought of her often and even more often since he moved back to Chicago. He tried to call her a few times, but he figured she had changed her number. He tried her at work one day, and they said she no longer worked there. He emailed her a few times, and she never replied, so eventually he just decided to let her be.

K.P. made it to Marcus's loft, reached over the door, and got the spare key. He knew Marcus would not be there because he was out of town with his fiancée, Tracy. He tossed his bag to the side and went to the fridge to see what Marcus had to eat. He grabbed a beer and the leftover pizza and hoped it wasn't that old. Marcus had only left the day before, so he figured it hadn't been in the fridge for too long.

He heated up a couple of slices, ate, and took a shower. Then he settled on the sofa and turned on the tube. He told himself to focus on the program and not the thoughts of Janiece that danced around in his head, but it was impossible to do. He finally fell into a deep sleep after replaying the last love scene of him and Janiece in his memory bank.

Chapter Three

Janelle Peoples

"Stop it, little boy, and eat your dinner," Janelle repeated. Her son had purposely dropped his fork on the floor several times to avoid eating his vegetables.

"But, Mommy, I don't like broccoli," he cried again, but Janelle was tired of hearing him say that.

"Greg, you eat it with cheese, so you can eat it without cheese!" she yelled, losing her patience. Her daughter, Gabrielle, had eaten all her food and bugged her for dessert.

"But, Mommy, I don't like it," he retorted.

"Fine, Gregory, get up. You do not get dessert," she said, snatching away his plate.

"Nooooo, Mommy, noooooo! I will eat it. Please, Mommy, I want dessert," he whined. Janelle set his plate back in front of him. He quickly stuffed his mouth, eating everything off his plate. Janelle then told him to go and wash his hands.

"Mommy, can I have my dessert now?" her daughter asked.

"No, Gab, I told you that you have to allow your food to digest, and if you ask me one more time, you will not get dessert, understand?"

"Yes, ma'am," she said and walked away with her head down. Janelle blew out a breath and put her hand on her head. She was exhausted and worn out. She looked at her clock and wondered what was keeping Gregory this time. He was working later and later, and she was tired of dealing with the children alone.

They were 3, not in school yet, and spent all day with Janelle because she worked from home. She'd take them to day care a couple of days a week so she could really get work done or when she just needed a break. Even though Greg insisted that she didn't need to, she hired a housekeeper to come once a week so the chores of deep cleaning and laundry could be taken off her list of things to do. Working, taking care of the twins, and trying to keep up with daily tasks, she had less time for herself. She was overwhelmed at that point, and Greg was not helping her lately with the kids. It was taking a toll on her.

After loading the dishwasher, she paused and gave the children a scoop of ice cream for dessert. After a little TV, she got them to bathe and put them down for the night. She went back downstairs to finish cleaning the kitchen and family room. It was after ten when Greg finally walked in. She was in bed when he walked into their room, and she instantly started in on him.

"Where the hell were you, Gregory?"

"I had a couple of drinks after work with the guys," he responded, loosening his tie.

"Why didn't you call me, Greg, or pick up your damn phone?" she yelled.

"Janelle, damn. I just walked in the damn door!" he yelled. "Can I at least take off my damn shoes before you start grilling me?"

"Gregory, please! What in the hell is going on? Are you having an affair? I'm not stupid. I watched Janiece date a married man for five years. I know the signs," she said.

"Janelle, stop!" he said and walked into their master bathroom.

She hopped out of bed and ran into the bathroom behind him. He was reaching in to turn on the shower, and she wouldn't leave him alone until she got answers.

"Well, what is it then, Greg? You go out almost four nights a week. You're starting to come home later and later, so is there someone else?"

"No, Janelle, no! I am not having a damn affair. Work is crazy, and I've been stressed. I have a lot on my mind, and every time I walk in the damn door, you hit me with this, that, and the other. I just need a minute sometimes away from this house," he said.

Janelle stood there wondering why he wouldn't just talk to her. "Well, say that then, Gregory. Don't you think I want to go out and relieve some stress too? The kids barely see you, Greg." She added, "They're in bed when you get home at night, and I don't like that."

He leaned back on the granite vanity and rubbed his temples. He was clearly irritated and didn't want to continue the conversation.

"Are you going to answer me?"

"I'm sure you do want to go out too, Janelle, and you can. I am tired of walking into a combat zone when I come home. I get tired of the constant complaining and questioning. You are twenty-four seven in my ear, which only adds to my stress levels. So I am saying it now. I want to come to peace."

She stood there, blinking in disbelief. He acted as if he didn't have to share any of the love of their marital issues. "Oh, so if I have a stressful day, I can't share that with you. If your kids have been driving me bananas all day, I can't express that to you because you need peace. Is that what you're saying?"

"No, Janelle, damn. Are you even listening to me!" he yelled. "There is no peace and quiet in this house, not one damn night of the week. Even if I'm home on the weekends with you and the kids, all you do is yammer about what is bad or what we don't have or what we need to do, or 'why don't you do this,' and, 'Gregory, when are you going to do this,' and I can't do that with you day in and day out," he blasted, and her eyes burned with tears.

"Oh, forgive me for burdening you with my day and feelings. Forgive me for sharing my day with you when you finally bring your black ass home. Maybe if you were here to cook, clean, bathe your damn kids, or even read them a bedtime story, I'd have fewer things to gripe about!" she yelled and stormed out of the bathroom but paused and went right back. She had more to say to him. "And!" she fired. "I'm fucking tired of touching myself to have a damn orgasm. I didn't marry my damn vibrator!" she spat and then stomped away. She entered her room, snatched the closet door open, and went for the quickest thing she could throw on. She settled on the sundress that was on the floor because she had missed the hamper. She quickly dressed, and Greg stopped her when she made it to the mudroom to put her feet into her sandals.

"Where in the hell do you think you are going at this hour?"

"To my sister's," she said and grabbed her keys and purse. Greg didn't stop her from leaving, and she was happy that he didn't dare try to convince her not to go. She needed space because she wanted to cuss him the fuck out, but what would that solve?

When she got into her car, she pulled out her cell and called Janiece.

"Hey, sissy," Janiece answered.

"Hey, what are you doing? I need to come over."

"I'm not busy, but what's going on? How are you out at this hour? What's wrong?"

"Everything. I'm stressed the fuck out with the twins, and I think Greg is having an affair."

"No way, Nellie. Gregory loves your ass more than he loves himself," she teased.

"Jai, he has been coming home later and later. He barely answers my calls or texts. When he does, he has lame-ass reasons for taking so long. Something just ain't right, sis, I'm telling you."

"Nellie, I hear you, but not Gregory. Greg isn't the type," she said, and that was what Janelle used to believe, but now she thought otherwise.

"Come on, Jai, what is the type? He's a man, so that makes him the type," she said.

"Well, I don't know. I just hope you're wrong. Come on over. Isaiah is out with some friends, so I'll open a bottle, and we will figure it out," she advised.

"Okay, sis, I will be there shortly."

Chapter Four

Janiece Lawton

"Isaiah!" she yelled when she walked through the door, and she got no response. "Babe!" she yelled again from the bottom of the steps, and still there was no reply. She walked back to the hall and opened the basement door. "Baby," she called out.

"Yeah, I'm down here breaking down these thousands of boxes," he answered.

"I got the test, so come on," she yelled. She had gotten a pregnancy test and couldn't wait to take it.

"I'll be right up," he said, coming up the steps within seconds. "Are you nervous?" he asked, following her upstairs to their master.

"Yes, are you?" she asked.

"Fuck, yes, but a good nervous," he replied.

After finally getting the box open and reading the quick instructions, she pulled away her jeans and panties and tinkled on the stick. She replaced the little cap and then set it on the vanity.

"Oh, shit, Isaiah, I can't watch," she said, pulling up her clothes. "I'm so nervous." She washed her hands and then peeped at the window, hoping and praying that the second line would come in, but unfortunately, it never did. After waiting the full three minutes and then some, they saw that it was still negative. Tears welled at the disappointment on the bathroom vanity.

He pulled her in close with a tight squeeze. But his hold did not elude the question. "Why is it so hard for us to get pregnant? We want to have a baby, but here we are, two years in with each other, and we can't conceive."

"Shhhhh, baby, please, no tears, and it is okay. We just must keep trying and stay positive. It will happen in His time, not ours," he said. "We just started trying since you've been off birth control, and the doctor specifically said it could take up to a year, so no tears, baby. Our time will come."

"I know, Isaiah, but this is still so depressing, and it hurts. It's been five months since we started trying, and I'm terrified it won't happen."

"Look, stop it, okay? We can't predict the future, which is so out of our hands, Jai. We just have to keep doing what we have been doing, and when it is our time, we will have a beautiful little replica of you or a handsome little replica of me," he assured her.

She grabbed the test and tossed it into the trash. "Yeah, I guess, babe," she said sadly. "I'm going to head to the condo and meet the cleaning service. What do you have in mind for dinner?" she asked.

"Anything you'd like, baby. It's like this moment is a bad moment, and as much as I'd like to say something to comfort you or make you feel better, I am at a loss. Just know that I love you, and that will never change."

"I know, and I don't need you to say anything different, because you are right. It won't make me feel better. I just have to ride out this wave, babe, and I'll be okay," she said with a smile before walking away. She wanted to have a full-blown breakdown but did not want to do that in front of him.

She walked down the steps, grateful that he didn't rush behind her with more kind words of encouragement. She knew it would come from a real place, but the reality was that sometimes she didn't want to entertain that shit. Sometimes she just wanted to wallow.

She got into her vehicle and took several deep breaths before she cranked the engine. It was what the fuck it was. She drove to her old place with thoughts of her future and what it would be like to have kids. With those thoughts, she made it to her old condo in no time. She got out and spoke to a couple of familiar neighbors before heading up to her unit. She noticed her nosy and irritating sister-in-law's car was gone, and she was grateful for that because she did not want to talk to Iyeshia at all. The longer she and Isaiah had been together, the more she disliked his sister, but she was always cordial.

Janiece got out, walked up the familiar stairs, and unlocked the door. It was hot as hell, so she hurried to the thermostat to turn on the air before she began to access the place. She made herself busy with social media until the space finally cooled down. She was snapping pictures with her phone of everything they'd have to fix when she heard a knock at the door. She figured maybe her annoying-ass sister-in-law had returned, but when she snatched the door open, it was K.P.

Everything inside of her quickened, and she had to remind herself that she was now happily married with her choice. "What . . . what the fuck?" she stuttered. "Why are you here?"

"I know, right? I am not here to cause trouble. Can I please come in?" he asked.

"No, and again, why are you here?"

"I just wanted to see you, check on you. I mean, it's been a long time, and I just . . ." he said, staring at her.

Now she was intrigued. "What? Wanted what?" she questioned, open to hearing what he had to say. She thought this conversation could be witnessed or even overheard by her sister-in-law, so she figured allowing him to step in would be better.

"Can I come in, just for a moment?"

She stepped back and let him in and then quickly shut the door. "Whatever you need to say, say it, and say it fast. Isaiah's sister lives across the hall, and I don't need any issues with my marriage."

His brows lifted to the ceiling at those words. "Married, Jai? You married him?"

"Yeah, two years now, so what do you want, K.P.? Why on earth are you here?" she asked nervously, hoping she wasn't physically shaking. Married and happy she was, but K.P. looked better than ever, and whatever fragrance he wore was hypnotic, and she was terrified to be alone with him.

"I had to see you. I just wanted to check on you to see if you were well, and I see that you are. And your place is empty," he said, looking around. "You moved, too?"

"Yes, we moved into our house a few days ago. I just came by to see what we need to prepare for the renters."

"Oh, wow, that's great, Janiece. I mean, you look beautiful and happy," he said, and she noticed that his eyes started to gloss over. Now he had to go because she could not have any emotional or heartfelt moments with him. K.P. was her past, and she loved Isaiah, so she had to cut the reunion off.

"I am, Kerry, and you should go because things are so good for me right now, and if Iyeshia sees you, she will have something to say, and I don't want to have to try to explain what and why," she said, and her eyes got a bit watery as well, so she looked down at the floor to stop having eye contact with him.

"I know, and you are right. No need to make waves for you and your husband. I just wanted to see you. Let you know that I'm moving back soon. I'm opening up a new location here, and I just wanted to catch up a bit, but I'll go," he said and reached into his pocket. He pulled out a card to hand to her, but she didn't take it, so he laid it on her countertop. She didn't say anything, so he turned and stepped toward the door.

"Moving back when?" she asked, and he paused.

"I have a few loose ends to tie up and close on my home soon, so I should be back for good by summer's end."

"Wow, that's great. Congratulations, K.P. I knew you'd be a huge success."

"Thanks, and congrats to you on everything."

"Thanks," she said, giving him a half smile.

They exchanged glances for a few more brief moments, and then he walked out the door. She went to the window to watch him get into a black Hummer and saw him slide on his shades before he cranked the engine.

When he backed out, he let down his window and looked up at her standing in her window. He smiled and then pulled away. He exhaled, swiped at the tears she finally set free, and took a couple deeper breaths.

She looked over at the card he'd set on the countertop, and then she picked it up to examine it. It was a business card for his brokerage firm. She tossed it back onto the counter.

She pulled her phone from her back pocket and called Janelle to tell her what had just happened.

Chapter Five

Janelle

"Noooooooo, Jai, are you fucking serious?"

"Yes, he just showed up and knocked on my damn door."

"What did he say?" Janelle quizzed, anxious for the juicy details.

"He just wanted to catch up and see if I was okay, and he said he is opening up a location here in Chicago and moving back."

"Moving back to Chicago? Oh, shit, shut up!"

"Yes, girl, when I say finer with time, that man is so damn sexy, Janelle. Why did he have to show his ass up to my place today? I hadn't thought about that Negro in ages, and he comes by here, clean, smelling good, and if I'm not mistaken, his damn shoulders looked broader."

"And how did it make you feel?"

"What do you mean? I don't want to feel or even think about feeling a damn thing for K.P. He broke my heart, and I refuse to allow him to come back and turn my world upside down. I am happy, and the only man I want is at home cooking me dinner. I'm trying to have a baby, Nellie. That's what I feel. I feel like loving my husband and having his babies. Seeing him was cool, but I won't allow any thoughts of K.P. fuck with my happiness."

"Well, I heard that. I'm happy to hear that you are K.P. free," Janelle said, and Greg walked in. "Listen, sissy, I need to call you back. My soon-to-be ex-husband just walked in."

"Nellie, you can't still be on that bullshit. You need to stop it. Gregory ain't messing around on you," she defended him.

"Yeah, whatever, bye," she said and hung up before Janiece could say anything else great about him. "Greg, I checked the account this morning and saw that you withdrew two thousand dollars," she said.

He tossed his briefcase onto the kitchen island. "And?

"And why?"

"Because I needed it," he said and loosened his tie. He then headed for the stairs, and Janelle was right behind him.

"Gregory, what did you need it for?" she yelled, running up behind him.

"Janelle, do I ask you to explain every dime you spend? You sit online and order hundreds of dollars' worth of stuff for you and the kids, and I never say a damn word, so if I decide to withdraw a couple thousand dollars to spend on something for me, I don't want to come home and have to explain it," he declared and walked away.

Janelle was tired of him being so damn secretive, so she decided to ask him again. "Greg, if there is someone else, you can tell me," she said.

He threw up his hands. She could tell he was tired of that subject, but she needed answers. "Janelle, for the last fuckin' time, I am not having a damn affair. I am not cheating on you, and I am tired of you accusing me of having a bitch on the side!" he roared.

"Then what is it, Gregory? You are so secretive about everything! You stay out late, and then you're not touching me," she cried.

He moved in closer to her. "Baby, stop, okay? Please, this has to stop. I'm tired of arguing every day about the same thing. I love you, Janelle, and I'd never cheat on you. I am under a lot of pressure at work, sweetheart, and that is it, that is all.

"I'm sorry that you feel I'm being secretive or creeping, baby, because I'm not cheating. I am exhausted from arguing and defending myself, and I'll tell you why I stay out late. I stay out late to keep from coming home and having another damn argument with you. I'm not excited to make love after you and I have been back and forth yelling and fuckin' screaming at each other. You wanna know why I took two grand out of the bank?" he said, going into his suit jacket pocket and pulling out a black jewelry box. "I took the money out to get these for you," he said, handing over the box.

She opened it to a pretty pair of diamond earrings. She covered her mouth and admired the gift because the little diamond studs were stunning.

"I wanted to come home and surprise you. Did you even notice how early it is? I wanted to come home and tell you to call the sitter so I could take you to dinner and give these to you, but the first thing on your lips when you saw me was, 'My soon-to-be ex-husband just walked in.' Before I say hello or ask how your day was, you are hitting me with why I withdrew money from the account. My goodness, how did my wife transform into a nag box?" he asked with stress lines drawn across his forehead.

Instantly she felt horrible and hadn't realized that she was the reason her man didn't want to be home or intimate with her. "I'm sorry, Greg, I didn't realize that I was that awful," she said, and a tear fell. "I'm just stressed a lot with the kids and work, and we don't spend time together like we used to before the twins and . . . I don't know, Greg, and I'm sorry, baby. I am." She sniffled.

He pulled her into a tight embrace and then kissed her wet cheek. "I know you are stressed, baby, and so am I, but I am not cheating. You are the only woman for me, but you are changing. You used to keep your hair done and wear makeup and dress so sexy for me. You used to want to have a good time and were always sweet to me, but after the twins, you turned grumpy, and I miss my pleasant, sexy wife. What happened to her?" he asked. He released her and then walked into the master bathroom.

She heard him start the shower, and then she sat on the bench at the foot of their bed and looked at the earrings her husband had given her. She decided she would have to stop being a nag and show him that she loved him. She got up, put the earrings on her dresser, and went down to check on the twins.

They were still in the family room, with toys everywhere, with one of their favorite cartoons playing on the screen. After making sure they were okay, she ran back up and stepped out of her clothes. She hurried into the bathroom and stepped into the shower with him. When he looked down at her, his dick immediately stood at attention.

"I'm sorry for how—" she tried to say, but he covered her lips. He slid his tongue into her mouth, and they exchanged a passionate kiss that they hadn't exchanged in a long time. He licked his way down her neck to her breasts and began to please her nipples. Her body remembered her lover, and her center reacted to his touch, and she felt her core contract. Her pussy was throbbing for her husband to penetrate her, so she leaned against the shower wall to balance herself as she lifted her right leg and wrapped it around his body.

Knowing what she wanted, he grabbed her by her ass and hoisted her up, and she wrapped her other leg around him. The tip of his dick was right there near her opening, so she pressed into him so he could slide inside. The look on his face as he entered her body was the look she missed, and she planned to do better. Within minutes they had a rhythm, and they both moaned and panted as her breasts bounced around to the beat of his stroke. Every stroke, every injection, made her pussy wetter and wetter for him.

"Yeeeesssssssss, baby, yesssssssssss, don't stop," she panted, and he pumped harder. The slapping sound of their skin was amplified by the shower's acoustics. When Greg's shoulders were hunched, that was his tell that he was going to explode, so she ground on him as he groaned out her name and squeezed her ass cheeks even tighter. Janelle held on tightly to his neck as she finished the ride. The dances stopped, and he held on to her for a couple of moments before he kissed her and let her down. They both panted and breathed deeply until their hearts returned to their resting beats, and then they lathered up.

When they stepped out, Greg grabbed his robe and offered to go check on the kids. They got pretty hot and steamy in that shower, and he wanted to ensure the kids were still in one piece. Once he was out of sight, Janelle gazed at herself in the mirror as she wrapped the bath towel around her body. Her curly mane was a bushy mess, and she hadn't had her eyebrows waxed in months. She looked down at her nails and toes and shook her head. Greg was right. She had let herself go. Since she worked from home, she rarely put on regular clothes. She didn't remember the last time she tried to get cute.

She called out to Greg, and when he came up, she asked him about dinner. He wondered if she still wanted to go out for dinner, and she agreed, but when she tried her sitter, she couldn't watch the twins. They ordered takeout, had a great evening laughing with the kids, and that night, bath time was painless because Greg was there to help her out. Once the kids were down, they opened a bottle, talked, and reconnected. They made love again that night, and Janelle knew she'd have to make some changes.

Chapter Six

Janiece

"Hey, babe."

She heard Isaiah's voice call out. "I'm in here," she called out from the kitchen.

He walked in with a stack of mail and a kiss for his wife. "Hey, beautiful, how was your day?"

"It was great, and yours?"

"Good. Went by the condo and got all the mail the new tenant was holding for us. You got it smelling divine. What are you making?" he asked and set the mail on the counter.

"Curried chicken, peas and rice, cabbage and cornbread," she told him.

He went to the fridge for a beer. "That's what's up, and yo' man is starving. I went by my parents', and my mom insisted that I eat, and I kept telling her, 'Janiece is cooking tonight, so I will wait.'"

She looked at him with the corner of her mouth curled. "So, you didn't eat anything at yo' momma's house?"

"Okay, I'm lying, but I still have room," he joked.

"I thought so," she laughed. "Speaking of family, yo' sister came by, and ooooh, she gets on my damn nerves." She cringed.

"Jai, what happened this time? Why can't you two just get along for peace's sake?"

"Man, your sister is always trying to run shit. She comes over to see our house since we are unpacked and settled in, and this heifer is in my house telling me what should go where."

"Say whhhaaaddddd," he said, and Janiece tossed the dish sponge at him. She knew he was half listening as usual when she griped about his crazy-ass sister. He knew their love-hate relationship, and he always had to referee.

"And get this, I leave her in the living room to get us wine, and when I go back, she has moved shit around like I wasn't going to notice," she said.

"Naaaaawwwwwww. I know you set her straight, didn't you, baby?" he teased as he went through the mail.

"You know I did," Janiece said with a neck twist. She looked over and studied the look on Isaiah's face. "Baby, what is it? What's wrong?" she asked with concern. He held up a finger for her to give him a moment to finish reading whatever he was reading.

"Fuck, fuck, fuck," he expressed and stood.

"Isaiah, what happened? Talk to me."

"It's my reserve unit. We are being deployed to Iraq. They are sending me back to Iraq."

"That has to be a mistake. Let me see that," she said, grabbing the letter. She read it, and although she didn't understand all of it, it was clear that he was getting deployed. "Baby, how can they do that? You're not active anymore. I don't understand."

"Janiece, even though I'm not active, I am still in the reserves, and reserves can get called to duty too."

"Okay, but this date is like six weeks away. Can you call somebody? Can we get a lawyer, Isaiah? This just can't be happening," she cried.

He pulled her into his arms and held her. "Listen, there is no one I can call and no choices in this matter. I am a soldier, babe, and I signed up for this, so this is what it is."

"So what do I do?"

He lifted her chin. "We make the most of these next few weeks, and then we have to separate for a while, and it will zoom by, I promise you."

"That's not what I want to hear you say, Isaiah."

He just pulled her back in and held her while she sobbed. "Listen, there is still hope, okay? Once I report and get more details, I'll know the facts. Deployments get deleted and changed, so there is still a chance that this won't happen."

That made her feel somewhat better, but not totally better. All she could do was pray. She went for the wine fridge and poured until the liquid hit the brim. She tried to focus on cooking but was so terrified that she just turned all the burners down to the lowest temperature and went out to the back patio. Before long, he came out and sat with her.

"You shouldn't worry, Janiece. This is not set in stone. I could get a letter tomorrow saying the orders were deleted or canceled. Just don't worry, sweetheart."

"I hear you, but what if they don't cancel it and you have to go?" She sniffled.

"Listen, bae, we'll cross that bridge when we get there," he said, kissing the back of her hand. After a few moments, she returned to her unattended pots on the stove and finished cooking. They both barely ate. They cleared the table in silence. They were on the sofa watching television, and although she tried not to cry, she kept batting away tears.

"Hey, come here," he said with his arms out in her direction. She moved over to him and got on top of his lap. "Do you remember when I had to leave and go back to Texas for those six months, and you were like, 'Six months is so long, and, baby, it's going to take forever,' but then it was like bam, those six months flew by?" he said, and she nodded. "Just think of it like that. It will go by in no time until that day comes. If we just love each other and stay positive and happy until if and when I have to go, we will be fine."

"You promise?"

"Yes, I promise, so please, just no more tears."

"Okay, I will try," she said with a smile.

"That's my baby. You are strong, and I need you to be strong for me and us. We got this. Whatever life brings our way, we got this."

"We do, don't we?" She smiled brighter. Isaiah always knew how to find a way to make her feel better. They talked more, and Janiece kept a positive attitude and promised she would stop with the waterworks.

The next couple of weeks passed, and when Isaiah went away for the weekend for drill, it hit her that she may have to have more than just a lonely weekend here and there without him.

The weeks rolled by with lightning speed. She watched him pack his gear for his tour in Iraq. There was absolutely nothing that could be done to stop this from happening.

She cried more tears that last week than she had in her life. She and Iyeshia drove him to the airport where he would fly out to Travis Air Force Base. She didn't want to let him go, but he had to go, so she forced herself to let his neck go. On the ride back, she just stared out the window. The tears wouldn't stop rolling down her cheeks.

"It's going to be okay, Janiece," Iyeshia said tenderly and grabbed Janiece's hand. She held her sister-in-law's hand but turned her face toward the window. "Time is gonna fly by," she said.

Janiece didn't want to hear another person say that shit to her. When she got home, Iyeshia came in for a little while, but Janiece wished to be alone. Iyeshia meant well but was on her last nerve. When she finally got ready to leave, Janiece did not stop her. She grabbed a glass and the merlot bottle and went to their bedroom. She got on their chaise with her favorite blanket and turned on the tube. She finally dozed off, and her ringing phone jerked her out of her sleep. When she saw it was Isaiah, she hurried to answer it. She was so happy she got to talk to him before he was on his long-ass flight to Iraq. When he had to go again, the tears flowed again.

That was only day one.

Chapter Seven

K.P.

Finally back in Chicago, K.P. was settling into his new home. As he unpacked, he came across a box he had forgotten all about, one he had never opened while in Vegas. It had lived in his garage, but it made a move back to Chicago with him, so he figured he'd finally tackle it and get rid of those things. There were photos and memorabilia from his five-year relationship with Janiece. It contained memories of the trips they had taken, keepsakes, and the ring he gave her that she gave back. He blinked back tears and thought back to the breakup and the final night they parted.

He thought about how he had treated her and gotten caught up with that bitch Shawnee, and he just closed the box. He set the ring on the coffee table and wondered if he should just toss the entire box, but then he just put it to the side. He got back to unpacking and tried not to think of her, but it was hard not to. It was too late to turn it off, so he went for a drink and told himself he'd get back to the unpacking business later. He went for a cold beer instead and went to sit on his patio by the pool. He looked at the beautifully landscaped oasis, looked over at his huge house, and felt lonely. He knew the kids would be home in a couple of days because summer break was ending, but he had no woman and zero potential.

He had dated back in Vegas but hadn't found anyone serious enough to bring back to Chicago with him. He decided then that he may want to incorporate dating into his life if he was going to find someone. He finished his beer and went back inside. He went over to his laptop and moved the mouse to go online to make a dinner reservation for himself, and a Facebook account popped up on the screen. He wondered where that came from and realized Kayla had an account.

"I told that child that she was too young for this crap," he said as he examined her stuff. "And you're eleven years old, young lady, not fifteen," he said, shaking his head and looking at the bogus year she had on her date of birth. He was about to deactivate her account, but something told him to search for Janiece. A few people popped up, but none was her. Then it hit him that she had to have a different last name, and he had no clue what that was. He then did a search for Janelle Peoples, and he found her page. As soon as he opened it, it showed Janiece Lawton under Relatives. He clicked on it and cringed a the Married to Isaiah Lawton under her relationship status. He started reading her posts and realized how many times she posted that she was missing her man and wished he was home. He clicked on Isaiah's page and saw a post saying, Finally made it to Iraq. Missing my baby already. He wondered what that was all about. He clicked on pictures and soon learned that Isaiah was in the army. That was shocking to him. He hadn't known that. He went back to Janiece's page and came across her latest post about going out to Jay's with her sister for a drink.

K.P. made a mad dash to the shower, and then he dressed. He topped off his look with Burberry cologne and grabbed his designer glasses. He drove his Mercedes CLS 550 coupe instead of that big-ass Hummer. He wondered how he would approach them and what he would say to her, and he prayed that she wouldn't cuss him out or slap his face.

When he arrived, he instantly became nervous and had second thoughts about going inside. He still hadn't figured out what he was going to say. He did a mirror check, took a deep breath, and got out. Once inside, he carefully scanned the room, looking for her. He didn't see her immediately, but moments later, he spotted her at the bar with Janelle. Then his smile faded because he remembered that Janelle hated his guts. "Fuck!" How was he even going to talk to Janiece with vicious-ass Janelle by her side?

He blew out a breath and said, "You're here now, and there is no backing down." He walked over to them as cool as he could because he was a ball of nerves.

"Janiece," he said as if he were surprised to see her. When Janiece and Janelle turned around, he felt like running the hell up out of there.

"K.P.," Janiece said, eyes wide.

"Yeah, I thought that was you. How are you? Hi, Janelle," he said, trying his best to play it cool.

"I'm well. I mean, I'm good, I'm fine," she stuttered.

"Great, and you, Janelle?"

"Hello, K.P. I'm great."

"You ladies look gorgeous. Can I get you two a drink?"

"No," Janiece said, but Janelle said yes simultaneously.

"What are you drinking?"

"Cosmos," Janelle answered. K.P. saw Janiece give her a look, but she turned back to him.

"Cosmos it is."

"Got it. I'll be right back."

"What the hell, Janelle?" Janiece said as soon as he walked away.

"What?"

"Do you remember who that is? K.P. The man you despised."

"That was way back when he was Kimberly's husband and you were his side piece. I have no reasons to hate him now, and, girl, you weren't lying when you said that he got finer, daaaayyyyyuuuummmm. Jai, that brotha looks delicious. I almost forgot I was married and he is your ex," she chuckled.

"Will you stop it? I don't want to be nowhere near K.P.'s ass. My husband is in the Middle East defending this country, and I'm sure he would not want to hear shit about me entertaining K.P., even if it is platonic. Go back to calling K.P. a low-down dirty bastard like you used to so he can get the fuck away from us," she said. She'd occasionally had a few thoughts of K.P. since they last saw each other, and she didn't want to play with fire. She was a good woman and a loyal wife. She didn't want to succumb to temptation.

"Janiece, calm yo' ass down. It's just a damn drink, not a dick. I know you aren't foolish enough to go back to him. If you are truly done and through, you should be able to be in his presence and be just fine. If you are truly over and done with him, being around him shouldn't matter. K.P. ain't no threat. You are married to fine-ass chocolate-ass Isaiah."

"Whatever. Cosmos," she mocked Janelle. "One drink from him and then he needs to move the fuck on, or I'm leaving."

"Okay, relax. He's coming," Janelle said.

Janiece rolled her eyes but smiled when he handed her the drink.

"Excuse me a minute. I've got to visit the ladies' room," Janelle said and got off her stool.

K.P. took the empty stool on the other side of Janelle. "So how have you been, Janiece?"

"Like I said before, I'm great. How have you been?" she said, and he could detect a little irritation in her tone.

"I'm good, finally settled into the home. The grand opening is next week, and it will be back to business as usual."

"That sounds great, K.P. I am happy for you," she said. They talked a little more, and then Janelle returned.

"Thanks for the drink, K.P.," Janelle said and then took a sip.

"My pleasure. How are things? What is up with Greg?"

"He is good. He's home with the twins."

"Twins? Get out. You have twins?"

"Yes, a boy and girl," she said and then took another drink. He and Janelle chatted it up, and Janiece barely said a word. Janelle went to take a call, and K.P. slid over to her stool.

"Where is your hubby tonight?" K.P. asked.

"Why?" she asked with her brow furrowed.

"Hey, Jai, relax. I'm just making conversation. I didn't think that you still hated me after all this time," he said and took a sip of his drink.

"I don't hate you, K.P."

"I can't tell," he joked and polished off his drink.

"He is in Iraq. His reserve unit got orders to be there for eighteen months," she said.

Her answer shocked him because he didn't expect her to tell the truth. "Eighteen months. That's a long time. How are you going to handle that?"

"I don't know. I don't have it all figured out just yet. I'm just taking it one day at a time. Just like when he was in Texas, and I had to wait for him for months," she said.

"Texas," he said and looked at her. He chuckled. "I should have known. That's where you went when you were supposed to have the training, right? When you couldn't be there for my grand opening," he said, looking at his empty glass and not at her. He shook his head and then waved for the bartender.

"Wow, K.P. I am so sorry for that. I'm sorry for lying to you, and I'm sorry for us not . . ." she said and paused.

"Johnnie Walker, please make it a double, and another cosmo," he said to the bartender. Janiece tried to decline, but he ordered it anyway. "Sorry for what, Janiece? You owe me no apologies. Our situations were fucked back then, and I got what I deserved."

"No, I wouldn't say that, K.P. None of us deserved the pain, drama, and heartache we all experienced, and I'm so glad that all of that bullshit is behind us," she said and polished off her drink. The bartender placed their new drinks on the counter.

"You're right, Janiece, and you know I wanted to spend the rest of my life making it all up to you," he told her.

She shook her head. "No, don't do that. I can't hear shit like this from you right now. I am married, so don't talk to me about what woulda or what coulda been. I don't need to hear that," she said and took a gulp of her drink.

He realized that he was upsetting her, which was the last thing he wanted to do. "Look, you are right, and I am sorry, but I need you to know that my biggest mistake was not leaving Kimberly when I met you. Not doing everything in my power to make you my wife fucks with me every now and then. I can't change the fact that you are married, and I can't change the fact that I will never have you again, but if I could, I would in a heartbeat. I'm so happy that you are happy, that's what I want for you, and I honestly wish you the best, Janiece. I know how lucky Isaiah is to have you," he said and downed his drink.

He stood. "Take care of yourself, Janiece," he said and leaned in to kiss her forehead. It was finalized. He had known that the last time he saw her, when she told him that she was married, but something in him thought that if she just saw him, she'd remember how much he truly loved her.

He ran into Janelle outside, and she was still on the phone. "It was good seeing you, Janelle," he said, stopping to say good night.

"You leaving? Did something happen?"

"Naw, I'm just way too late. Coming back to Chicago was like coming back and winning her back, but I fucked that all the way up, so I have to find a way to let it go right," he said.

"Sadly, but yes. She is happy with Isaiah, and he is a great husband. I knew there was a time when I could not stand the sight of you, but you know what, K.P.? I get now that marriage is fucking hard, and I judged you so harshly when I had no clue what you were going through."

"Thanks for that, Janelle. You ladies get home," he said and proceeded to his vehicle.

He said to himself, "Well, K.P., it's time to find a new love and get over the old one."

Chapter Eight

Janiece

Janiece stayed in bed late again that morning, in the dark, with her black-out curtains closed. It had been a month and two days since Isaiah left, and all she did was sleep her days away. She talked to him on the phone in the late evenings, and they Skyped in the wee hours of the morning for her, and although she tried, she still couldn't remember the time difference. Isaiah noted in the last video that he didn't like how she alienated herself and that she looked super sad. He said he wanted her to cheer up, maybe go back to work or even work at his dad's dealership so she could get out and not mope around the house. He told her he understood that being apart was hard, but he didn't want her depressed about it.

She agreed for argument's sake, knowing he was right, but she was too deep in her funk to entertain reason. She dragged her lazy-ass body out of bed and went to the bathroom. She looked at herself in the mirror and had to admit she did not like what she saw: hair matted, puffy eyes, and a look of sadness that she didn't want to keep carrying. Her skin was amazingly clear, prompting a little grin before she grabbed her hairbrush. She spent way too long detangling, she thought, but it had to be done. Once she made a ponytail on top of her head, she grabbed her face towel. She was dead set on removing all traces of her puffy eyes. She alternated hot and cool towels on her face.

By her third time allowing the water to run over the towel, a full rush of nausea hit her out of nowhere. She swallowed hard to suppress her queasy feeling and the lump that was swelling underneath her tongue. She took a seat on the side of the garden tub. She took slow and easy cleansing breaths to keep herself from vomiting, but that did not work. She rushed over to the toilet, and she let the eruption happen. Her body jerked as last night's contents decorated the porcelain bowl, and she gagged as her body tried to give more, but there was nothing left. She grabbed some tissue from the roll to wipe her mouth and eyes because the puking caused tears to fall. She flushed and then just sat on the floor to regain her composure. After a few moments of deep breaths and sniffles, she grabbed more tissue and blew the explosion's remains from her nose.

She crawled over to the side of the tub and hoisted herself up from the floor. She then stood in front of the mirror and examined herself. She wondered what had brought on the nausea and why she still felt lightheaded. She brushed her teeth and gargled, and then she went to get dressed. She had a couple of errands to run and a care package that she needed to mail to her husband.

She dressed, went about her day, and then grabbed her favorite Italian beef combo from Portillo's since she was on that side of town. When she got home, she tossed it into her toaster oven to warm it and then took the extra cup of gravy she ordered and poured it over it to get it nice and wet like she loved it. She wasted no time inhaling it and decided to do some cleaning.

She had neglected everything since he had gone, but she wanted to get back to normal and back to living, maybe even work at the dealership. Her father-in-law had asked several times for her to come in to work in their finance department. She was always good with numbers, which was her background, but when she finally left her job, she and Isaiah decided that she would be a stay-at-home mom. Although the mom part hadn't happened, she was a stay-at-home wife.

After cleaning her living room and master, she hit her master bath. The kitchen didn't need much because she hadn't cooked a meal since her husband left, but she wiped down everything, vacuumed, and mopped. She was about to head down to the basement to tend to the laundry when she stopped in her tracks. A wave of queasiness returned, and she shook her head side to side rapidly because she did not want to throw up. She'd had a great Italian beef combo and was on her third glass of Moscato, so she did not want to vomit.

She swallowed and swallowed and swallowed hard, but before she could get to the bathroom, she decorated her hall floor with wine and beef chunks. She fell back, sat on the steps, and wondered what was happening. She missed Isaiah, yes, but nausea and vomiting had nothing to do with missing your husband, and then it hit her. She realized she hadn't had her cycle since before Isaiah left. She rushed up the steps, went into her master bedroom, and made a beeline to her master bath. She snatched open the bottom drawer to retrieve the extra pregnancy test that came in the box of two.

She ripped open the test and then sat, and within seconds her body gave her urine. She put the cap on and put the stick on the vanity. She wiped and then stood, and within less than a minute, two lines appeared. Janiece could not believe what she was seeing. *Pregnant.* She was finally pregnant.

Her lips curled into a smile as happy tears welled in her eyes. This was the happiest moment she had had since Isaiah got on that plane to leave. Involuntarily she screamed and then ran in place. She was so happy, and all she wanted to do was tell Isaiah he would be a dad, but she couldn't. She didn't have access to just call him. She'd have to wait for him to call her, and Lord forbid if that would be days. She held the stick close to her chest and thanked God so many times, and then she thought about Janelle. She didn't have many people to share her news with, but her sister would be the first. She ran down for her cell and into the mess she had created in her hallway, so she decided to clean that up first.

After making the hall Pine-Sol fresh again, she went for her phone and called Janelle.

"Hello," she answered groggily.

"Hey, sissy, were you sleeping?" she asked.

"Nah, baby sis, I'm up," she said, but she didn't sound like herself to Janiece.

"Well, what's wrong, sissy? You sound like something is wrong."

"It's nothing, okay? Don't worry, babe. Yo' big sissy is okay," she replied, but Janiece did not believe that. She knew Janelle, and she was always in good spirits. For her to sound so dry was different.

"Come on, Nellie, I know that voice. You are not okay, and I'm here, so spill it."

"Janiece, listen. I am okay, and nothing is going on that you need to be concerned about. Don't worry. How are you? How is Isaiah?" she asked.

"Well, last I heard from Isaiah, he was good, and I am good and pregnant."

"What!" Janelle yelled into the phone.

"Yes, I took the test, and I am pregnant, sissy. After all this time, I am finally having a baby, and I can't wait to tell Isaiah."

"Wow, Jai, honey, that is wonderful news, and I am so happy for you. I knew you two would make me an auntie."

"Oh, my God, Nellie, it just feels so surreal, you know? It seems like a dream, and I have to wait until my husband is allowed to call me to tell him, and that really sucks, you know? I just wish he were here." She sniffled.

"I know, sis, but at least it happened. You will have this great news when you talk to him."

"Yeah, I know, and I am bursting. It's like I want to see my baby bump already. I mean, I am having a baby," she squealed loudly.

She and Janelle talked for a long while, and she got off to try to eat a little something again. She looked at her wine bottle and glass and laughed because there would be no more indulging. She decided on salami, cheese, and crackers. She hoped it would stay down. She grabbed a blanket and got comfy on the couch with her Kindle. She went to look for baby books and expectant mommy books, then she dozed off. She heard her Skype ringing, and she sprang up from the sofa. Her laptop was on the dining room table, so she hurried to answer.

"Hey." She smiled brightly.

"Hey, gorgeous," he replied. "You look amazing, baby, and I miss you so much," he expressed.

"Thank you, baby, and I miss you too, more than you know, handsome," she returned. "How are you?"

"I'm perfect now that I see your beautiful smile."

"Well, I have a reason to be smiling, babe."

"Oh, yeah? Enlighten me. I don't want you sad, but your face is glowing right now, babe. What changed your mood? The last few times we talked, your eyes were puffy, your face was sad, and now you look so radiant."

"Well, something great happened today, Isaiah."

"Okay, are you going to share it with me?"

"I am, hold on," she said and raced up the steps. She had forgotten to bring the test down. She sat back down and took a deep breath. "Close your eyes," she said.

"Really, Jai?" he asked.

"Yes, really," she insisted. He did, and she put the stick in focus on the camera. "Now open them," she said.

"Baby, no fucking way," he replied, leaning in close. "Janiece, please, baby, don't play with me."

"It's not a joke, Isaiah. You are going to be a father, and we are having a baby." She beamed.

"I . . . I am at a loss for words. I'm going to be a dad, baby. This is so great, and I am so happy, my love. I just want to hold you and kiss you right now, baby. This is the best news ever, and I am bursting."

"You're happy, Isaiah?" she asked, knowing the answer.

"Hell, yeah! Did you tell my family? My mom is going to be thrilled at this news."

"No, I wanted to tell you first," she said, not telling him that she had told Janelle.

"Wow. I mean, do you know how far? When is the baby due? I mean, when are you going to the doctor?"

"Well, I am going to talk to Janelle. She had a great doctor for her and the twins. Then I will go from there. But I'm guessing I'm a little over a month along because I had my last period maybe two weeks before you left. But I can't be sure."

"Okay, just get to the doctor soon. I hope I can take R & R around the delivery time. Hell, who knows? I am just happy, baby, and I love you more than I've ever loved anyone in my life, Janiece."

She smiled. "And I love you right back, Isaiah, and I am so happy. Being away from you is hard, baby, but I'll get through it. Your baby inside of me gives my heart so much joy, and soon you will be home, and we will have our baby, and things will be perfect," she said, and the tears fell.

"Ahhhh, babe, don't cry, okay? We are having a baby, and that is enough to keep you smiling while I'm defending our country," he said.

She smiled and didn't give him any more negative talk. They talked for a few more moments, and then his time was up. She stared at the screen moments after he was gone and then got up. She immediately started to think of names as she climbed the stairs to go to bed. That was the first time since he had left her that she didn't cry herself to sleep.

The next day, Isaiah's family was on her line with a million and one questions that she couldn't answer. She hadn't seen the doctor yet, so she had no clue when she was due, how far along she was, or if it was a boy or girl. They expressed their happiness, and she knew they would be happy to have their first grandchild.

She made her first appointment, and after she was seen damn near two weeks later, she had answers to everyone's questions. She tried her hardest not to go on social media with the news, but she was so happy, so she posted her announcement along with the ultrasound photos of her baby. News traveled fast, and she received a ton of congratulations from family and friends.

Chapter Nine

Janelle

Janelle dialed Greg's phone again, and he didn't answer. She sat there, took another sip of her wine, and wondered what his excuse would be this time. No matter what he said, his actions were speaking louder than his words. She knew he was lying and fucking around on her. She went online and logged on to her bank account. She looked at the last few transactions and saw several restaurants and adult spots on the statement at least two or three times a week. She wasn't the one going out to those places.

She was getting nowhere, and she felt helpless. She quickly thought of Diamond, Greg's hot assistant. She had to check her a couple years ago because she thought she had a touching problem. She'd find a way to touch Greg on the arm, the shoulder, or the knee, and Janelle went off one day when she walked in and caught her giving her husband a neck massage. Of course, Greg being a fool in denial said that it was innocent, and Janelle told him that, innocent or not, she didn't want Diamond's hands on him ever again.

She knew it was a fat chance that she'd get a straight answer, but she called her anyway.

"Hello," Diamond answered. Her voice was sexy and deep as it had always been, and Janelle felt foolish at that moment. She wanted to hang up, but she cleared her throat and spoke.

"Hey, Diamond, this is Janelle. I'm so sorry to call you so late, but I can't seem to get in touch with Gregory. I was supposed to meet him at dinner tonight, but I can't seem to find the note he left for me. I've called several times, and I assume he is busy, but I'm already tardy," she said as calmly as she could. She was a ball of nerves, hoping that Diamond didn't catch on that she was lying.

"Ummmm, let me take a look at his calendar. Can you give me a sec?" she asked, sounding more professional to Janelle's ears. She figured the last impression of her weighed on Diamond, so she had to let the past go and respect that the reason Diamond was still there was because she did great work. "Okay, he has a client meeting tonight with Kelley Michelson at Hotel Dana, downtown on North State Street. If you don't want to be crazy late, I suggest you head there now, Mrs. Peoples," she said with concern.

Janelle had never liked her, but she smiled. "Thanks so much, Diamond, and I'm headed there now."

"You are so welcome, and have a lovely evening," she added politely.

Janelle hung up, her heart racing. What was she going to do? Show up uninvited? Hell, she had to see what was going on for herself, so she called Janiece to ask her if she could look after the kids for her. When Janiece agreed, she got off and went to get as pretty as she could in a short time. It was five to seven when she left, and she was sure she'd miss the entire dinner by the time she made it downtown.

After the valet took her vehicle, she walked in, confident that she was doing the right thing. All she wanted to do was save her marriage and confirm that Greg was true to her, but things went way left. She immediately spotted him at the other end of the bar with a gorgeous woman and another gentleman. The woman sat in the middle of the two, and just like with Diamond, Janelle noticed the woman had a hand on her husband's thigh. She took a seat and signaled for the bartender. Greg still hadn't noticed her presence, and he must have been having a great, humorous conversation with the two, because he was laughing at whatever they were discussing.

She hadn't seen him laugh in a long time, but she turned her attention to the bartender who approached. She ordered a drink, and he was back in a jiffy with her order. She sat there for almost ten minutes sipping her drink, and not once did Greg even look her way or notice her sitting there alone. He was so engaged with the two people he was with he hadn't looked around. After a few more moments of hoping he'd see her, she waved for the bartender again. That time she ordered another drink and sent a Scotch on the rocks to her husband. When the bartender pointed her out, she smiled at him, but he did not smile back. His face did not say, "Hey, baby, I'm happy to see you." It said, "What the fuck?" A look of dissatisfaction was written all over his disgusted face. She knew that he was not happy to see her the way his black man's look of dismay graced his beautiful brown face.

Janelle wanted to bolt, but she had come so close to what she needed to know, so she sat up taller in her chair. She needed answers. She saw him say something to his counterparts before he headed her way.

"What the fuck, Janelle? Are you serious right now? You're poppin' in on me?" he asked, facing her with his back to his fan club.

"Well, hello to you too, husband. I mean, I can't get a proper greeting? I'm the mother of your only two children," she spat, trying to keep her composure.

"So it has come to this? You're following me now? Spying on me?" he asked through tight teeth. He was trying his very best, she assumed, to keep his voice down.

"Who is she, Gregory?"

"She is a client I am trying to bring over to Harris Bank, and it is not a good look for my wife to just show up like she is out to catch me cheating or having some kind of damn affair." He looked at Janelle with rage written all over his face. She had never seen his nostrils flare or his lips tighten that way since they exchanged I do's, but she was not going along with that wack bullshit he said.

"You are telling me to my face that she is a potential client and you're trying to solicit her business for the bank, but you can't introduce her to your wife, the mother of your children? Is that what you are telling me right now?" she asked him, and at that very moment, she wanted to slap his damn face.

"Yes, that is exactly what I am telling you. If I had arranged a dinner date with her to meet my wife, you'd get an introduction, but since that is not the case, I am not going to take my insecure wife over to meet her. That is not a good look for me, Janelle. If my wife can't trust me, how in the fuck would she trust me with her fortune? So for that reason, I need you to leave." His tone was firm and direct, and she knew her marriage was done.

She sat there and peered at the lovely woman talking to the other gentleman who sat beside her. Her husband had no intention of introducing her to either of them, so she blinked back her tears, swallowed the rest of the contents of her glass, and then stood. "Good night, Mr. Peoples, and please enjoy the rest of your evening with your potential client." She didn't wait for a response. She just hurried to the exit.

When the valet came back with her car, she was barely holding on to her tears. She got in and began to sob loudly. She never thought she'd be the one to be cheated on by a man she loved so much. Greg was so good to her, her best friend, her mate, her everything, but now that was all gone. A horn honked loudly behind her, so she wiped her face and pulled away.

She drove with nowhere to be, and she didn't want to go home. She pulled off the expressway and into a gas station to think for a moment. She pulled out her phone and texted Janiece to check on the twins, and when she replied that they were already asleep, she knew she wasn't going to go pick them up.

She pulled down the visor, went for her makeup bag, and began freshening up her face. She had to get herself together and get something going on for herself since her husband had his whatever the fuck going on. She thought about just going to Janiece's and crying her eyes out to her, but then she said fuck that and decided to head to Jay's. She parked, and before going inside, she took off her wedding rings. She put them into her purse and then got out.

Once inside, she hurried over to the first available stool that she saw. She ordered a cosmo, and the woman who was sitting beside her vacated her seat. She wondered if it was because she sat down, but she decided not to give that shit much thought. She grabbed the drink as soon as it hit the bar top and downed it. She asked for another and told herself not to let a tear fall. Her heart was broken, but she didn't want to be a sobbing bitch at the bar.

By drink number three, a baritone voice interrupted her thoughts. "Is someone sitting here?" he asked.

She looked over her shoulder and saw a masterpiece, so she shook her head side to side. "No, no one is sitting there," she managed.

He took a seat, and the bartender was there in a flash. "What can I do you for, Devon?" he asked.

"Aaaayyyeeee, Tony, my man, what's crackin'?" he asked, and they shook.

"Nothing much, man, just managing shit now. You know Julian has been home way more since the twins, and I'm here more than I'm home."

"Welp, somebody got to do it, huh?"

"You know it. Henny and Coke?"

"And you know it," the stranger replied.

"I got you, man," the bartender said and went to fix his drink.

"What are you drinking?" he asked Janelle.

"I'm sorry?" Janelle said, taken off guard. She was too busy eyeing her phone, wondering if she should text or call Greg.

"What are you sipping on, beautiful?"

"Oh, a cosmo. That is still my go-to."

"Cool, I got your next one. I'm Devon, by the way. Devon Vanpelt," he introduced himself, extending his large hand.

She shook it. "Nice to meet you. I'm Janelle. Janelle Hawkins," she returned, using her maiden name.

"Nice to meet you, Janelle," he said and ordered her another drink when the bartender came back with his.

"Thanks for the drink," she said when it was placed in front of her.

"No problem, pretty lady," he said, and she smiled. "It's kinda slow for a Tuesday night, huh?"

"Well, to be honest, I wouldn't know. I don't come here much during the week."

"Thursday is usually a good crowd if you decide to come back on a weeknight."

"I'll keep that in mind."

They continued to make small talk, and he offered to buy her another drink.

After a couple of silly jokes on the other patrons who graced the space, he asked, "So where is your husband?"

"I don't have one," she lied quickly. "Where is your wife?"

"I'm divorced," he said. "My first wife, I messed up big time, and my second wife left because she said I couldn't let go of my first wife, which was kinda true but not true, so I don't have a wife."

"Are you still not over your first wife?"

"Yes, I am over my first wife. She is married, has three children with him, and we have a daughter together. Deja is now twelve and the only woman in my life." He smiled.

"Okay, I can understand that," she said and debated if she should mention the twins. She declined that, and they continued to talk.

It was close to two a.m. when Devon offered to walk her to her car. "Thanks so much for your company and for walking me to my car."

"It was my pleasure," he said and opened her car door. She prayed he wouldn't ask her for her number, but he did. "I'd like to call you," he said.

"Listen, I just met you, and I am kinda taking a man break, but I'll tell you what. The next time I see you, if things are different, I will give you my number."

"Okay, Janelle, I can understand that. That is the cleverest way of telling a brotha no, but I can dig that," he said with a smile.

"No, I didn't say no. I just said next time." She got in, and he closed her door. She cranked her engine, and he walked away.

She rolled down her window. "Thursdays are good, right?"

He smiled. "Yes, Thursdays are lit."

She nodded and then drove away. She didn't care if Greg stayed out late anymore because she had plans to do the exact same thing.

Chapter Ten

K.P.

He was standing in his new office building, smiling at his success. He thought back on where he started and was grateful that he ended up as financially successful as he was. He had it all but Janiece. He knew no money in the world could take her place, and he missed her every day. He found himself on Facebook every day stalking her page, and when he saw her post about being pregnant, he could have had a heart attack. As the days went by, he wished it weren't so, but by the time she was showing, she posted pics of her baby bump, and he knew it was real.

According to her most recent post, she was four months pregnant, and he still could not stop thinking of ways to get her back. His brain worked overtime on ways to win her back, but the reality was that she was gone. Moved on and happily married with a baby on the way.

He sat down at his desk and did something he knew would probably get him cussed the fuck out, but he did it anyway. He grabbed his phone and called Janelle. He still had her number from years before when he was their closing agent for their home. He just hoped it hadn't changed.

"Hello," a woman answered, and it was Janelle's voice.

"Hey, Janelle, how are you?"

"How did you get this number?" she asked, and he heard the panic in her voice.

"I've had it forever. Is this a bad time?" he asked.

"How did you get my phone number?" she asked again.

"Janelle, this is K.P. I've had this number since I helped you guys close on your house."

"K.P. Oh, my goodness, man. I thought . . . never mind. Why in the hell are you calling me?"

"Relax, I don't want any trouble. I just want to check on her. I am no longer in her life, but I miss Janiece so much. Is she happy? Is she truly good? I just have to know if she is happy. And even if so, I need to talk to her. I just want to hear her voice. Is there any way that you can convince her to call me?"

"Listen, K.P. I know you miss her and all that jazz, but Janiece is so happy right now. She is having her first baby, and things are good for her, and she is in a happy place. I mean, I can't mess with that. You are like a part of her that needs to stay asleep."

"I know, but, Janelle, I wish I didn't love her so much. I wish I could let her go every day and let her be, but I miss her. She was exactly what I needed, but I was just . . ." He paused. "I just wish I had made my moves sooner."

"I know, K.P., but my sister is happy, and I'm sorry I can't help you," Janelle said.

"I understand more than you know. And I honestly do wish her well, and I am truly happy that she is happy," he said, and his eyes watered. His words were sincere and true, but he hated that he had lost her for good.

"I know, and just know that Isaiah is one of the good ones, and she is in good hands."

"I don't doubt it," he said sadly. He gazed at the picture on her social media page that he had up on his laptop screen, and he blinked back more tears. "Take care, Janelle, and please save this number. If she needs anything or if he steps sideways, call me at any moment. I don't care if it's night or day. If she ever needs me, I'm right here." Janelle agreed to save his number and call him whenever she felt Janiece needed him.

He wrapped up and called it a day. When he got home, it was uncomfortably quiet. The kids were with Kimberly, and K.P. was single and now alone. He grabbed the controller to his audio system and turned on some smooth R&B. He then grabbed the remote to his gas fireplace and turned it on. Before going to his master to undress, he poured himself a stiff drink. He had to get back to living and get over Janiece. He needed some head and some pussy at that point, so he had to make himself available and meet some new prospects, but by the time he was in his loungewear, he was back on the sofa with thoughts of Janiece. His mind would replay all the fun times they shared when he could make her happy. How simple gifts would put a huge, beautiful smile on her face, something he could never do for Kimberly. He knew it was shitty now, but buying two of the same gift didn't seem foolish back then. He remembered how Janiece would be over the moon, and Kimberly would just turn up her nose.

"Man, you fucked shit all the way up," he said aloud and then got up to pour himself another drink. He ended up back on the sofa with more memories of the past, and his eyes burned because none of them deserved the bullshit they went through, not him, Janiece, or Kimberly. They all suffered a great deal of pain, and now Kimberly's spoiled, rehabilitated ass was with Rodney, and Janiece was with the man she chose over him when it was all said and done. He was the one who had lost love and hated that he still loved her so much.

He downed his drink and decided to go get dressed. He would head out to Jay's to at least find someone to warm his bed. And from that night on, he was on a mission to get over Janiece.

Chapter Eleven

Janiece

It had been almost a week since Janiece had last heard from Isaiah. It was not like him to go that long without a call or email, and she was worried out of her mind. She called his mother ten times a day, hoping they had heard something, but every time it was the same answer: no, not yet. She wondered how his family was so relaxed about it, but her sister-in-law kept reminding her that they were accustomed to how it worked when Isaiah was deployed. Sadly, Janiece wasn't. She was on pins and needles with worry and wasn't sleeping at night, afraid she'd miss his call or Skype.

After much convincing, Janiece decided to relax and just pray, and with that, she finally fell into a deep sleep on the sofa. The Skype ringing woke her, and she popped up so fast that her laptop hit the floor. She quickly retrieved it and answered it. As soon as she saw him, she began to sob.

"Hey, baby, why are you crying?" he asked with concern.

"Oh, my God, Isaiah, I have missed you so much, and I have been worried sick, baby. What took you so long to call? I've been worried out of my mind."

"I'm sorry, beautiful. Trust that I miss you so fuckin' much too, baby. I know you were worried, but the internet over here was down, and there's been craziness going on, but don't worry, babe. I'm good, okay?"

"I see, but I was so scared," she cried. "I just want you home."

"I know, sweetie, but I won't be too much longer. If you don't hear from me, just don't worry or think the worst. You are carrying our baby, and you need to relax," he said, and then the screen froze.

"Okay, I get it, and your screen is frozen again, babe. How are you? Tell me the truth, Isaiah. How are you doing over there?"

"I am good, darling. I'm good. I think about you and the baby when I am off duty. Let me see your stomach," he said, and she quickly turned on the lamp. She lifted her tee for him. "That's my baby girl, growing strong, and your belly is beautiful. I can't wait to rub it and feel her kick and move."

"Well, I'm just starting to feel more movement. It's light, but I feel her moving around more often now."

"We are almost at week twenty, right?"

"Yes, we are, and you are a great dad for keeping track. I mailed a box for you yesterday. Your mom made your favorite cookies, and I got you a little something, something in the box, too." She smiled.

"Oh, I wish it was your . . . you know," he said, but he was still frozen, so she couldn't tell if he was making any gestures.

"Oh, how I wish I could mail it to you too, babe, but it will be something to make you smile, love."

"I can't wait. I have to go now. It may be a couple of days before you hear from me again, but promise me that you won't worry, Jai. I am okay, and your man is good."

"Okay, Isaiah, but please promise me that you will be extra careful for the baby and me."

"Yes, I promise, and I promise to love y'all forever."

"We love you too, babe, forever."

"I miss you, and I will talk to you as soon as I can. I want to name the baby Jaiden, so think about it. I hope you like it," he said, and before Janiece could respond, he was gone.

She repeated the name a few times and smiled because she liked it. She remembered when she found out it was a girl. She sent him a package with pink everything to celebrate that they were having a girl, and he was over the moon. The first thing he'd said was, "Now I'll have two girls to love and spoil," putting a huge smile on Janiece's face.

She took a screenshot of the frozen image of him, and then she put her laptop on the table. She felt better now that they had spoken, so she climbed the stairs and got into their bed. She grabbed his pillow with his cologne and held it as she drifted off to sleep.

The next morning, she woke, and when she checked her emails, Isaiah had sent her a short message and a couple of pics of him and his army buddies. She looked at the pictures over and over again, and then she made breakfast.

The next few days were quiet, but she didn't worry herself as promised. She prayed, let God do His job, and just busied herself with baby stuff. Iyeshia and Janelle were at her house trying to paint the nursery while they sipped wine and giggled. They were of no help, but now five months pregnant, Janiece was determined to get some of the painting done. Her belly was bigger than she thought it would be at five months, but she still managed to get a couple of coats of paint on the wall.

They were laughing and joking when the doorbell rang. Janiece figured it was Tia since she was supposed to have come a couple of hours ago, so she sent Janelle down to answer it. "Janiece," Janelle yelled, and Janiece went down to see what was happening. She saw two uniformed men, and one had a folded flag in his hand. Her heart raced when she approached the door because it instantly dawned on her why they were there.

"No, no, no, no, no, no, no," she repeated over and over again.

"Janice Lawton," one man said.

She continued to cry out, "No, please no."

"What's going on?" Janelle asked.

"We need to speak to a Janice Lawton," he said.

"It's Janiece, and I am her sister, Janelle. This is Janiece," she said. By then, Janiece was leaning against the wall, holding her stomach with a frightened look plastered on her face. Iyeshia came running down the steps and immediately knew, but Janelle was apparently still confused.

"I'm so sorry, ma'am, but we need to talk to Mrs. Lawton," he said.

"Let them in," Iyeshia said as she helped Janiece to the couch. Her face was already wet, but she held it together as she sat next to Janiece. The two men came in and introduced themselves by name and rank, and they told Janiece that Captain Isaiah Earl Lawton was killed in the line of duty. Janiece could not hear the sobs of her sister and sister-in-law over her own. She screamed loudly and was glad her sisters were there when she got the news.

She calmed down enough to try to hear what the uniformed men had to say, but she only heard "invasion," "explosion," and "what is left of his remains." All the other details hadn't really registered. She nodded at other instructions that they gave her, but she knew she wouldn't retain any of the information because her husband was dead.

Numb, she lay on her sofa and let Iyeshia and Janelle make phone calls. Within an hour, her place was full of loved ones and friends, and she just wanted to be alone.

By the time the house was clear, only she and Janelle remained. She had no words, only tears. That was all she could do.

Her husband was dead. *Dead after fighting for a fucking country that hates us*. He was gone. "Janelle, you don't have to stay," she said.

"I know, but I am," she replied.

"No, go home with Greg," she insisted.

"Greg is going to take the twins, and I'm going to stay here with you," she said and then got up. Janiece couldn't even lift her head. She just stared at the wall and let the tears have their way. She held her belly, and eventually, she fell asleep.

Janelle came back to check on Janiece and thanked God that He allowed her to fall asleep. She was in her own feelings about her tired husband. She'd called him fifteen times, but he didn't answer. She had to text him that Isaiah was dead for him to call her back, and she had to restrain herself from cussing his ass out the entire evening. She knew it was bad timing for Janiece, so she didn't address the bogus shit she had going on with Gregory.

She sat on the love seat and tried to fall asleep, but she could hear her sister moaning in her sleep. She wasn't sure if she was awake and crying or feeling her emotions in her sleep, and she didn't want to upset her with questions. She got up, went for her phone, and stepped outside on the patio. She knew Janiece would most likely cuss her out, but she called the one person she knew her sister may need.

"Hello," K.P. answered.

"Hey, K.P., it's Janelle, and I am sorry to wake you," she said because she could tell from the grogginess in his voice that he had been awakened.

"No, it's fine. Is Jai okay?" he asked, and she could detect the panic in his voice.

"It's her husband, K.P. Isaiah was killed," she sobbed.

"Oh, nooooo. Janelle, how is she? I am so sorry to hear that. How is Jai?"

"She is finally sleeping, but she will need all the support she can get. She may cuss me out for calling you, but she may need you, and I thought you should know. If she just needs you to hold her or listen or send food because she is stubborn, please say you will. She is pregnant, and I will be here as much as I can, but I have a whole situation going on with my marriage, and mentally I am going through it, so will you be here for her?"

"Listen, Janelle, you know how I feel about your sister, so you know I will. Just let me know when and what, and I will be there. And whatever you got going on, I'm here. I'm no expert, but I can be an ear. I know marriage is hard, so whatever you are going through, consider me a friend, Janelle. Shit ain't easy, this I know."

"Thanks, but my concern is for Janiece, so be on stand-by. She will need a lot of support, especially with the baby."

"I got you. Like I said, whatever she needs."

Janelle finished up the conversation and sat for a moment. She was going through enough, and now this. She was on the verge of a mental breakdown, but she had to be a fake wife and a big sister. She was miserable but had to keep pretending all was good.

She went back inside and made herself comfortable on the loveseat. Janiece was finally softly snoring and into a sound sleep. Janelle said a long prayer, as she had been the last few months or so, but she felt her prayers were bouncing off the ceiling because she and Greg were not getting better, and they had drifted further apart. She was entertaining another man she was growing to like, and her world was upside down. Finally, she drifted off to sleep.

The next morning, she was awakened by a frantic Janiece screaming.

"Nellie, Nellie, I had the worst dream ever. I had a horrible dream," she cried, and Janelle was looking at her teary-eyed. "Janelle, tell me it was a damn dream. Tell me that last night did not happen. Please tell me that it wasn't real. Please," she begged.

"I'm sorry, sissy. I'm so sorry," Janelle said, letting the tears fall.

"My baby. Isaiah. Isaiah. Oh, my God. Isaiah. Nellie, he is gone. How can he be gone!" she cried louder. "What do I tell our daughter, Nellie? This can't be real. Please tell me I dreamt it, please," she cried even louder.

Janelle rushed over to hold her sister, but she didn't want to be touched. "I can't . . . can't breathe, can't swallow right now. I . . ." she said and ran to the bathroom.

Janelle stood outside the door and listened to her sister vomit, moan, and cry, and she slid down the wall. She had no idea how to care for her sister, but she was determined to figure it out.

Chapter Twelve

Janiece

The memorial service was packed, and Janiece didn't know half the people there because she and Isaiah were only married for two years. She never attended many family functions with him, and his parents handled most of the arrangements because Isaiah never changed over his benefits package when they married. They told Janiece they would cut her a check when the military gave them a full payment, but that was the last thing on her mind. She and Isaiah had a policy, but the military would ensure that she and the baby would be okay.

She held Janelle's hand tightly as many came over to offer their condolences. She nodded with a half-smile and wished they would just leave her alone. She was a pregnant widow, and she just wanted to go home and cry herself to sleep. Iyeshia was driving her crazy because she acted like she was Isaiah's wife and wouldn't shut her damn mouth. Janiece understood that they shared a womb and all their bath times and blah, blah, blah, blah when they were kids, but Isaiah was her husband. They were married and shared something more sacred than any relationship.

When they got to the burial grounds, Janiece sat and watched them lower an empty casket. She wailed because she couldn't even bury her husband's body. After the ceremony, they threw roses into Isaiah's empty grave. Even though his body wasn't in that expensive box, Janiece was frozen and couldn't bring herself to leave. It was like that would be her final goodbye to the man she called her husband, and she was too emotional to walk away. Everyone had gone but Janelle and Iyeshia, and as they tried to make her get up, it was no use.

"Listen, we can't drag your pregnant ass to this car, Janiece, but if we have to carry you, we will," Iyeshia barked.

"Just give her a few more moments," Janelle insisted.

"Is that yo' ex?" Iyeshia spat, and they both looked over to see K.P. "The fuck is he doing here?" Iyeshia barked.

"Relax. I called him," Janelle declared.

"For what? How in the fuck do you call that nigga? Are you for real?"

"This ain't about you or me. This is about Janiece. He is a friend, so I called him," Janelle barked back.

"You know what? Whatever! She was never good for my brother," she spewed.

"Don't you even go there, Iyeshia," Janiece said, looking up at her.

"No, fuck that you let this muthafucka come here. Are you fucking him now?" she yelled, standing over Janiece.

She shot up out of her chair. "Are you fucking for real? Fuck you, Iyeshia, fuck you! You have no idea what I am going through. Your family has no clue because no one asked me what I wanted for my husband's homegoing. Y'all just dove in, and I had to sit in silence while y'all took over everything. I love my husband, and he is dead! I didn't even get to say goodbye to my husband or send him off the way I wanted to, so fuck you. Think what you want to think about me and K.P. and whatever else you want to think. Fuck you!" she blasted.

"Fuck you too! You lying whore, bitch. You will not keep my brother's baby, and I promise you that you will see how we treat whores like you," she returned, and she marched away. She went to the car and rolled away.

"She is truly a piece of work."

"Yes, but why did you call him, Janelle? Why?"

"Because he is a friend, and you need him."

"I don't."

"You do," she said, and then Janelle waved to K.P. to come over.

"Hey," he said when he approached.

"Can you please take me away? I need a moment of peace," Janiece said.

He reached for her hand. "Of course. Whatever you need, I am here."

Chapter Thirteen

K.P.

K.P. and Janelle helped Janiece into his Hummer, and he drove Janelle home first. He looked over at Janiece, who had a face full of tears. He did not know if she wanted to go home or to his place. "Jai, where do you want to go?"

"Anywhere but home. Someplace quiet, where I do not have to hear a ringing phone or anyone asking me how I'm doing. I don't want to see another flower or hear another person tell me how fucking sorry they are," she cried. "I just want to be left alone for a whole minute and have some damn peace. Just a few moments of peace," she proclaimed, and he drove out to his house.

He got her settled into his bed and then called Kimberly. He asked if she could manage the kids for a few days, and she agreed. Although she lived thirty minutes from their school, she assured him they would be good.

K.P. checked in on Janiece several times. She was in such a deep sleep that she was snoring. He lay on the couch, turned on the television, and made sure the volume was low.

The next morning, he walked in and was shocked to see her awake so early. He went over and grabbed the remote to open the drapes to let the sunlight in.

"Why did you come?" she asked in a hoarse voice.

"I don't know, to be honest. My first thought was that I'd upset you, but then I thought you may need me, and I don't know, Jai. I just had to check on you."

"I don't know what I'm going to do. I honestly don't know what I'm going to do next, not even in the next fifteen minutes or the next hour," she cried.

"Well, don't do anything. You can stay here as long as you need to. I will get you whatever you need, Jai. Just let me help. I am clear that this is not about us. I just want to help you be okay, and when you are ready to go back, I'll take you back."

"Thank you. I honestly needed to get away from everything and everybody," she said with tears falling.

"Listen, Jai, whatever you need, I am here. Don't worry about a thing, sweetheart. I'm going to make you some breakfast. There are fresh towels and a robe in the bathroom for you. Janelle called and said she'll bring some clothes for you and things from your house, so no worries. We got you."

She nodded. The baby started to move, and she touched her stomach. "She will never know who he was. She will never have the pleasure of knowing how great her father was. That hurts me to my soul."

"I know it must be hard, Jai," he said.

"You have no fucking idea how horrible this feels."

"Listen, I'm going to go make some grub. You should take a bath and let it relax you. The tub is enormous," he added.

"I will." She began to sob.

He wanted to walk away, but he went to sit next to her. "You will be okay, Jai, in time, I promise."

"Kerry, I just can't see it. I can't see beyond today and right now. The shit hurts so bad, and I can't see it."

He pulled her close and held her. "I know, but give it time. I remember when your dad died, Jai. You were devastated, but it got easier, and this will too."

She nodded, knowing his words were true, so she encouraged him to go and allow her to take a bath. She was relaxing in the tub and rubbing her stomach when he tapped on the door.

"It's open," she said.

He stepped in with the phone. "Janelle is on the phone," he said, handing the phone to her. He had seen her naked hundreds of times, so she didn't feel uncomfortable with him seeing her body in the tub.

He told her the food was almost ready and exited the bathroom. She talked to her sister and told her the things she needed from her place. She got off, cleaned her body, and then got out. She grabbed the robe hanging on the hook, put it on, and let her nose lead her to the kitchen.

She wasn't familiar with the layout of his home, but she managed to find her way to the kitchen. On the way, she looked around. His place was exquisite, and she loved how beautifully decorated it was. It felt warm, like a cozy, luxurious hotel or something grand like that, yet homey. She admired everything about it and wondered for a moment if Kimberly lived this extravagantly when he was married to her, but she quickly shook away those thoughts of their horrific past.

"Have a seat," he offered. She went over and struggled a little getting on the island stool, but after a bit of maneuvering, she was good.

"Your house is so beautiful. I'm looking around like, wow," she said, looking out the large patio doors that graced the entire left side of the kitchen. "And you have a pool?"

"Thank you, and yes. The kids made it clear that they would not leave Vegas unless we had a pool in our new place, so I hunted until I found a place with a pool for them."

"Humm," she said with a smile. "When did you learn how to cook good, Mr. Paxton?" she asked, eyeing the food he had prepared for her. When they were together, he never cooked one single meal.

"Single parenthood. When I took the kids back to Vegas without you, I had to feed them. I purchased a couple of cookbooks, took some classes, and learned to cook a few things so Kayla and K.J. wouldn't grow up on burgers, fries, and pizzas."

"I see," she said with a sigh. She did feel bad for checking out at the end and not going through with their original plans. "And you know I am really sorry for how things ended with us."

"I do, and I hope you know how sorry I am for all the hurt and bullshit I put you through," he said, putting her plate down in front of her.

"I know," she said and then said a quick prayer over her meal. She was starving at that point, so she quickly shoveled a forkful of eggs and grits into her mouth. She nodded as she chewed. "K.P., this is really good."

"Thank you." He smiled.

She went for the French toast and didn't say much more until after her plate was clean. "That was delicious. I haven't eaten much lately, and I needed that."

"I am glad you enjoyed it," he said, taking her empty plate. "Listen, I just opened the new branch here, and there is still a lot to be done, so I must go in for a few hours tomorrow. I want you to stay, so if you need me to hire someone to cook and stay with you for the next few days, just say the word."

"No, I'm fine, and I can manage. I am just so glad to have some peace right now. I know my in-laws are cussing me out, and I know Iyeshia has given Isaiah's parents the embellished version of yesterday's events and our history, and I just can't deal with them right now. As long as there is food for me to feed my little one in my womb, I'll manage. Janell is bringing me some things from my house. I just need a couple of days of silence to recuperate. Right now, I am just so drained and heartbroken. I'll face them later."

"You don't have to face them alone. I'll be by your side if you need me to be."

"I know you will, but it's complicated enough. I appreciate you showing up yesterday and just being here for me now. My in-laws just kinda transformed into strangers. They just took over and acted as if I didn't love him or I had no say, and I . . . I don't know what things will be like now. Iyeshia seeing you is like atomic, so I just need to stay here a few days to breathe, grieve, and figure out what is next. After that, I'll let you get back to your life."

"Back to my life," he said with a little chuckle.

"What?"

"I mean, you're not an interruption on anything, and I don't want us to go back to being strangers again. Drop you off and never see or talk to you again is not what I want."

"K.P., I can't offer you anything right now. What good would I be as a friend? I just lost my husband, so I just need a minute, and if that's too much, I can go home now because after I leave, I don't see a need for us to be in contact."

"Are you serious?"

"I just don't want things to get confusing. I am not here with thoughts of us getting back together."

"Do you seriously think that's on my mind right now? I'm here for you because, regardless of what we've been through, I still care about you, Jai. No crazy ideas are circling around in my head. I'd never prey on you when you are in such an emotional state, so please don't read my being here for you as a way to get back with you. I'm not a perfect person, but I'm not that kind of man," he said and walked out of the kitchen.

She sat there for a few moments, thinking about what she had just assumed and that it was not cool of her to think that was his motive when he was only trying to be there for her. She got up and went to a few doors until she found him. He was in his office.

"Can I come in?" she asked from the doorway.

He looked at her and then gave a nod.

She came in and sat in the chair in front of his desk. "I am sorry for what I said. I know you are not a creep, K.P., and I am sorry. I am grateful that you are here for me right now. You are a great man to even have me here after our history, and I am sorry. Now that Isaiah is gone, I don't know what is what. I just know that you are the only man I've ever loved besides him, so I don't want to"—she paused to think—"I don't want to rebound with you. I figured if we go back to not talking, I'd move on and not just run back to you for convenience or our history, so if you are good with me staying here with no desires to be with me, I believe you."

"I'd never lie to you and say that I feel nothing for you, because I do and may always feel what I feel for you. However, you are safe to grieve, be you, move on, fall in love again, or do whatever you choose to do. I can handle us being friends."

She smiled. "I'd like that."

"Now get out of my office because I have a ton of shit to do," he teased.

"Damn, friend, okay," she said and stood.

"I'm just fuckin' with you, but you are welcome here as long as you need to be, and whenever you are ready to go home, I'll take you home. We should run out this evening to get a few items because the kids have been with Kimberly for a few days, and it's kind of bare. I'll set your things up in the guest room when Janelle gets here. The keys to the other two cars will be here, and I'll give you a proper tour a little later."

"Sounds good. Now I'm going to go check for ice cream," she giggled.

"That I do have," he confirmed, and she vacated his office.

She went for the ice cream, and then she decided to explore. She knew he would give her a tour, but she just looked around.

Janelle came with her things and stayed a little while with her. She ended up on the sofa, and she dozed off. He woke her, and they went to the store for groceries and ordered takeout for dinner. She was good until she powered on her phone. She had back-to-back alerts, and the Lawtons were definitely pissed at her.

Chapter Fourteen

Janiece

A month had gone by, and she managed not to cry every fifteen minutes. She was down to a couple times a day, and now at seven months, she felt huge and irritable. She was home, and she had not touched anything of Isaiah's. She left all his things in his drawers, and all his clothes and personal items were still in their places.

Isaiah's parents talked to her occasionally, but she could sense the tension, and Iyeshia hated her. She assumed that she and KP were back together, which wasn't true. He called her every day to check on her, but she hadn't seen him in almost three weeks because she knew it was better for him to stay away. She was not mad at K.P. for being so sweet to her, but she hated that he was because she felt like she was doing Isaiah wrong for being friends with the man who caused so much drama and pain for her.

Every single time he made her smile, she felt guilt. Every time he sent her flowers or had her favorite food delivered to her out of the blue, she felt guilt. He continued to ask to see her, and she kept telling him no because she knew it wasn't right, and she was still mourning and crying for Isaiah. He was dead and gone, and as much as she asked God not to let it be, it certainly was what it was. She had no clue how she would continue without him, and with a baby girl on the way, she wondered how she would raise her baby without her father.

When she walked out of the building from her doctor's appointment, she was greeted by a man holding a sign with her name on it. Confused, she asked, "Who are you, and what is this?"

"Are you Ms. Janiece Hawkins-Lawton?" he asked like he was confirming it.

"I am," she replied.

"Mr. Paxton sent me to take you to a few stores to purchase some things for your new bundle," he said with a smile.

"I'm sorry?" she asked as if she were confused, but she wasn't.

"He sent me to take you baby shopping, and he said if you said no, he'd understand."

She hesitated but did not say no. She smiled, got into the car, held her tummy, and rode silently. She got out at the first store, and the saleswoman called her by name and was eager to assist her. She didn't go crazy and kept it light, but the saleslady informed her that she had no limit on what she wanted. Janiece still shopped modestly and didn't do much damage. After cashing out and confirming the delivery address, they rolled to store number two. Again, she was greeted by name and smiled because she hadn't shopped for the baby, and money was getting tighter since Isaiah's parents hadn't given her any of Isaiah's insurance money.

She first tore the clearance rack up and then moved over to the things she knew she wanted for her baby girl. By store number four, she was exhausted, didn't want to pick out another pink or yellow outfit, and was hungry. Before the car pulled off, her phone rang, and it was K.P.

"You are doing too much!" she said when she answered.

"Hello, Janiece, how are you?" he returned.

"Hello, and why are you doing all of this?"

"Because I know you, and I know what you need. How was your day?"

"Exhausting. I've never been tired of shopping in my life, but I'm drained. My feet are swollen and killing me," she expressed.

"That much shopping, huh?"

"Yes, a good friend of mine thought it would be nice to shower my unborn baby with a few needed things, and her mother is grateful. Thank you so much, K.P."

"You are welcome, and just sit back and relax. I will see you soon." He hung up, and Janiece instantly realized that the driver wasn't taking her back to her vehicle.

They pulled up to K.P.'s house about twenty minutes later, and he got out to open her door. He helped her out, and she waddled to the front door. He let her in, and she followed him into the kitchen, where the aroma of something good invaded her nose.

"Take off your jacket, put that purse down, and give me some time to finish preparing dinner for us," he said. She did what he said and sat at the set dining table instead of the island. Before she could settle in, a woman approached.

"Hi, Janiece. I am Sylvia, and I need you to come with me."

She looked at Kerry. "What's going on?"

"Just go, please. This is all about you," he said. He looked defeated in that kitchen, so Janiece just went with the older woman.

Once in a room she had never been in, she was handed a robe. The woman told her to undress and that she'd be right back. She looked at the massage table and almost pumped her fist in the air because she needed this. After she had undressed, she sat and waited for the woman to return, and when she did, she offered assistance to get on the table.

"I'm almost eight months, ma'am. I can't lay on my stomach," Janiece expressed.

"I know, and this table is made for expectant moms. There is a hole here," she said, pointing it out, "where your tummy will be comfortable." With that, Janiece allowed her to help her get on the table and into a comfortable position.

The massage was a glorious hour, and afterward, Janiece joined K.P. in the dining room for the meal he'd cooked for them. There were candles, and it was romantic and nice, she thought when she sat.

"K.P., this is all so nice. You have gone through so much trouble to make this day special for me, and I appreciate it."

"You deserve it. And I hope you enjoy this meal. It's my second time making it, but I think I did well."

She cut into her chicken, tasted it, and gave him a nod. "This is good. You did good," she said. "This is too much. Why are you doing all of this? We agreed to just—" she tried to say, but he cut her off.

"We are friends. There are no strings attached to any of what I do for you. I know Isaiah's family has been treating you shitty, and you are trying to keep it together. Sometimes it's not what you say, it's what you don't say, and I know you are stressed, Jai."

"I am, but I feel horrible when I am around or talking to you. I feel like I'm cheating on him, like I'm giving my marriage to him the finger because I am right back here with you. Isaiah was a good man, Kerry, a good man, and he loved me, took care of me, and was so good to me. Every time I'm near you, I feel horrible because you make me feel good, and I wish you didn't. I feel like I'm cheating on him with you. I can't explain it. I just feel like I am horrible to him whenever I am smiling with you," she confessed, and tears welled in her eyes. She loved

Isaiah, but K.P. was her first love, and she did not know how long she could fight the urge to be back with him.

"Jai, I never want you to feel guilty for our time. Isaiah died, which is horrible, babe, but he is no longer here. Life has to go on, and I'm not trying to tell you to stop mourning or grieving. You do all of that at your own pace, baby, but I will be right here waiting with open arms when you are ready. Our thing isn't dead, and I will respect your time and give you all the space you need. I'd never try to erase him from your life. I love you, and I'm right here, and I will wait, Janiece, I will, and I am a patient man. I just need you to be true to yourself and stop worrying about what his sister thinks or his parents say. They are where and with who they want in life. And if you are not ready, baby, I am good. I'll wait, and if you never come back to me, I will have to live with that," he said, and she let the tears fall.

She heard, believed, and felt him, but it was too soon. She was torn because she loved them both so much, and she wasn't ready for K.P. She still longed for Isaiah.

"And just ask yourself this one question," he said. "If you died that day instead of him, would you want him to love again or just be alone?"

"I'd want him to love again," she whispered.

"What do you think Isaiah would want for you?"

"To be happy and to love again. He was a great man, and he'd want me happy," she said.

"So stop feeling guilty when I make you smile. You can't feel guilty forever, sweetheart. If something makes you feel good, let it. You didn't die with him, and when you love someone, you want the best for them. You want them happy," he said and moved over close to her chair. He was on a knee in front of her, and she leaned in and cried on his shoulder. He held her tight, and she just released. He had been a great friend and made sure every single day that she was okay. Only love would make a person do that. Yet still, she wasn't ready. "Don't worry, Jai, you will feel better in time," he said, kissing the side of her head. He wiped her tears, and she allowed him to kiss her lips.

The kiss turned into another, and then she closed her eyes and allowed him to kiss her passionately. She released, and K.P. kissed her the way he did when they first met, and as soon as she began to enjoy the kiss, the baby kicked, and she pulled away. "No, no, no, K.P. I shouldn't be here. I shouldn't be doing this with you. It's too soon. My husband just died, and I need to leave. Take me home, please. I can't," she cried, trembling.

"Okay, Jai, babe, relax, it's okay. There is no pressure, and I'll take you home," he said, standing.

She got up and dressed and was standing by his front door in a matter of minutes. She shook at the thought of what she was doing and rubbed her tummy insanely. She got into his Hummer, and they rode in silence. She rubbed her belly, asking her unborn child to forgive her. She spoke to her baby in her mind saying how much she loved her father. When he pulled up at her house, she went inside and rushed to the bathroom. K.P. unloaded all the baby items that she had gotten earlier that day. He was on his last bag trip when Iyeshia pulled into her driveway.

"Awww, hell," Janiece said.

"What in the hell are you doing at my brother's house?" Iyeshia blasted as soon as she got out of the car.

"Excuse me?" K.P. replied like Iyeshia was a nobody.

"You heard me, muthafucka. Why are you here at my brother's house?" she yelled again.

Janiece rushed over to get between them because she knew it would be a bad scene if her voice rose any higher. "What the hell, Iyeshia? Why are you out here yelling in my driveway?"

"No, bitch, please explain why this ma'fucka is coming out of my brother's house. What the fuck is he doing here, Janiece? Why is this nigga all up in my fam's crib?"

"This is my house, Iyeshia, and it's none of your damn business what goes on in my house. Why are you even here?"

"Janiece, I'm gonna go. Everything you need is in the house, so I'm going to go now," K.P. said. "Unless you need me to stay."

"Yes, I need you to stay until she is off my property," Janiece said.

"Oh, you feel threatened by me and want me to leave my bro's property. This is my brother's house, bitch, and my brother has been dead for, what, thirty-seven days, and you got this nigga here? Is that even my brotha's baby inside of your damn womb? Huh? Is this bastard the real father?" she questioned, looking at K.P. "The jig is up, bitch, and I got you. You never loved my brother. You've always had a thing for this white-collar bitch, and my family gon' handle yo' ass fo'sho," she said and finally got back into her vehicle. She pulled out of the driveway and peeled off.

Janiece stood there shaking. She couldn't believe what had just happened, and she questioned the baby. All she had tried for her entire marriage was to get pregnant, and now the only thing she had left that was a part of him was in question. "K.P., what in the fuck just happened?" she said, watching Iyeshia's taillights disappear from her street.

"I don't know, baby, I don't, and I got a feeling things are about to get ugly."

"Ya think?" she said, encouraging him to go inside. She sat, and she just dropped her head. "I lost my husband, and nobody fucking gets that," she cried.

"I'm sorry, Jai," he offered.

"No, K.P., you've done nothing wrong. Shit is just all the way fucked up now."

"Are you going to be okay?"

"No. I need to pack a bag and return to your place. They are not going to leave me alone or grant me any peace. I am damn near eight months pregnant, and they don't care, K.P. When Iyeshia goes back to them with this, I know it's gonna be bad, so can I go back with you?"

"Of course, for as long as you need."

Chapter Fifteen

Janelle

"What time will you be here?" Devon asked.

"Well, I'm going to head home and shower and change, so in about, let's say, a couple of hours," Janelle replied.

"Okay, just call when you are on your way."

They ended their call, and Janelle drove home from the salon with a huge grin on her face. She had gone out with Devon a dozen times and was starting to really like him and love his company. She felt guilty at times, but when Greg didn't come home for dinner like he promised or ignored her calls all day, it eased the guilt. She had no clue how her marriage would make it, and at that point, she didn't give a shit and gave Greg the same energy he gave her.

When she pulled into her garage, she was shocked to see his Benz. That was odd, but she was still going through with her plans with Devon. The smell of something delicious penetrated her nose as soon as she stepped through the door. He was cooking, to her surprise, and she couldn't remember the last time he had done that. She hated that it smelled so damn divine.

"Hey," she mumbled and put her purse on the island.

"Hey, babe," he said, looking her up and down with a pleased smile. She knew she looked good after her trip to the salon, so she welcomed the once-over.

"You're home early, and cooking, too," she added.

"Yeah, I picked up the twins, told the sitter that we didn't need her today, and decided to go ahead and get dinner done since you were still out."

"Okay," she said, stepping out of her shoes. She was happy to see him making an attempt, but that was just a small gesture. "I am going up to shower," she told him and headed for the stairs.

"It will be done soon, so hurry back down," he yelled after her, and then she paused in her tracks before going up the steps.

"I won't be having dinner with you guys tonight. I have plans, and I'm going out."

"Where? This is the third night this week, Janelle," he questioned.

"Oh, we're counting now?" she returned with a hand on her side and tilted head.

"No, but that is what it is," he answered, and she knew his statement was legitimate.

"Well, I already told Janiece I was going, so I am," she established with a look that she knew he wouldn't challenge.

"Okay, Nellie, if you already made plans, you have plans," he said and went back to cooking.

She headed up the steps and stopped to greet her twins with hugs and kisses before she made her way to her master. She went to her closet, scanned through her dresses, and pulled one out while praying she could fit into it. She had been working out and was down twenty-five pounds since she had started, but she had more weight to shed.

After that, she selected her accessories and then went to shower. She quickly applied a little more curl control to her moist hair. She had just gotten it done, so it was easy to manage, and it was not the bushy mess she was used to after her showers. After she moistened her skin with her favorite scented lotion, she stepped into her thong. She put on the matching bra and looked at herself in the mirror.

Not bad, she thought for a woman who simultaneously carried two kids in her womb. She went to her vanity and got started on her makeup, and just as she finished, her husband entered.

"Wow, you're getting pretty dolled up for a dinner date with your pregnant sister. Are you sure your plans are with her and not someone else?"

She looked up at him in the mirror. "Gregory, don't come up in here with that mess. I'm not the one . . ." she said and then paused. She didn't want to argue. "After dinner, I may meet my girl Trina for a cocktail," she said.

"Cocktails with Trina?"

"Yep," she said and then blotted her lips. She tossed the tissue into the wastebasket and then stood. She went for her dress and then stepped into it. "Can you zip me up?" she asked, hoping it would zip. He zipped it slowly and pressed his nose against the back of her neck.

"You smell good," he said, kissing her gently on her neck. He roped an arm around her waist and pulled her into him. She let him hold her for a few moments and then walked out of his embrace. "And you look stunning," he complimented her. At that moment, she started to feel horrible for what she was doing.

"Thanks, babe," she said and gave him a smile.

"I'm gonna head back to check on the twins and see what horror of a mess they are making in the kitchen," he said and then quickly vacated their master.

Janelle stood in the mirror and had second thoughts about going to Devon's, and then her phone sounded. It was a text from Devon.

Devon: Can't wait to see you!
Janelle: Leaving now.

She headed down the stairs and paused when she saw her family at the kitchen table eating and laughing with each other. She missed that because Greg was never home at dinnertime, and she wished this wasn't a once-in-a-while thing. His weekends became busy, and he wouldn't come home until the late-night hours.

She interrupted, "Hey, little ones, Mommy is leaving now," she said, moving to kiss her babies. She went to Greg and gave him a kiss too. "Bye, babe. I'll try not to be too late," she told him.

"Okay, have fun, my love, and be careful. Tell Jai I said hey," he said. She agreed that she would.

She grabbed her coat, purse, and phone and made her exit. She got into her car, and her nerves jumped all over the place. She put her wedding rings in her armrest and then put Devon's address into her GPS. When she arrived, she didn't get out of the car right away. She took a few cleansing breaths and then told herself that this was what she wanted to do. She approached his building with fear, thinking she should turn her ass around and go back home to her family, but her feet kept moving in the direction of his building. She stopped by the desk, and the young lady gave her a look when she gave her Devon's unit number and name. She rang his unit and gave Janelle more attitude when she said she could go on up.

"The elevators?" Janelle inquired because she had never been to his place. The clerk nodded with a point, and Janelle smiled at her, even though she didn't return one. She chuckled at the young lady and went on about her way. What her problem was was not Janelle's concern. She rang the bell when she got to his door, and he quickly opened the door.

"Hey, gorgeous," he said when the door opened.

"Hey, handsome, and thank you," she said as she entered. He quickly helped her out of her trench and hung it for her.

"You are most welcome, and I hope you are hungry," he said.

"I did bring my appetite, and whatever you are cooking smells so good," she added.

"I'm almost done. You can have a seat if you like," he said as he made his way to a dining room table set for two. He pulled out a chair for her. She put her purse down on the sectional that was near her and went to take a seat. He went into the kitchen, and she looked around his space. It was a bachelor pad, and it was decorated well, in gray, black, and white with a splash of burgundy. It was done well, she thought. It was spotless, and she was happy that he had an inviting home. He appeared with a plate that he put in front of her.

"Wow, this looks and smells good, but I need to wash my hands first."

"Sure, of course," he said and gave her some quick directions. She went and tinkled first, and after she washed her hands, she stood at the vanity and told herself to relax and enjoy him. She was only doing exactly what Greg was doing. *Just relax.* She returned to join him, but he hadn't touched his food.

"Why aren't you eating?"

"I was waiting for you," he said.

"Oh." She smiled and then bowed her head. She said grace and grabbed her fork and knife.

He made grilled salmon, rice, and mixed veggies. They ate and exchanged plenty of conversation. When they were done, she helped him clear the table. Once they were in his tiny kitchen, he convinced her to let him load the dishwasher and put away the food. She sat on the barstool on the other side of his small peninsula, and they continued nonstop conversation. "Where did you learn to cook?"

"My ex-wife, Leila, taught me a thing or two. She is an amazing cook."

"Why do you always smile when you talk about Leila?"

"Do I?"

"Yes, you do," she replied.

"I didn't realize. She is just so special to me. She is my daughter's mom and just an amazing human being. After all the bullshit I put that woman through, she has never kept me away from my daughter. And we just have an amazing friendship now. There was a time when I thought she'd hate me forever. It just took us a long time to be where we are, and I have the utmost love and respect for her. Even Rayshon and I have bonded over the years. It took us so long to get here. They are not only my friends. They are my family, and if I smile, it's also because I am finally where I am supposed to be with Leila, Rayshon, Deja, and the other kids. We are just closer than we've ever been."

"Interesting," Janelle commented and took another sip of her wine.

By then, Devon was done loading the dishwasher. He opened a wine fridge underneath the counter that Janelle hadn't noticed and opened another bottle. He topped off her glass and then his. He invited her over to the sectional. It was massive, and she got comfortable in the corner of the left L-shaped cushion. He sat and immediately pulled her feet onto his lap. At some point, she had removed her shoes after dinner to get more comfortable.

"What about you, Janelle? Do you want to get married or have kids?" he asked.

Her heart started racing because she knew the words dripping from her lips would be more lies. "Yeah, maybe, someday," was all she said, hoping he didn't have any family follow-up questions.

"Well, I plan to get married again and want more children. My ex-wife Christa . . ." he said with a chuckle. "Even if we had made it, I doubt she would have given me children."

"Why do you say that?"

"She is, I mean, a famous model, and I could barely get her to eat bread. She was too concerned about her waistline, so I knew she'd never ruin it for a kid."

"Wow, that is funny."

He cleared his throat, and his tone became serious. "So, Janelle. What are you looking for?"

"What do you mean?"

"Are you looking for love, dick, or taking it slow? Are you just out here dating?"

She giggled. "Well, I'm looking for happiness," she said, keeping it simple. She was married and unhappily married, and she just wanted to feel good. She did not reject or resist him when he leaned in to kiss her.

He took her glass, set it on the coffee table, and returned to her lips. He was a great kisser, and he was gentle but passionate. She fell into a rhythm with his touch, and her body began to respond to his kisses. The electricity between the two of them was real, and she wanted to climb on top of him and grind against him. She lay back on the sectional and allowed his hand to go up under her dress and onto her thigh. Things grew more intense when his fingers found their way to her clit and opening. Her mind said to get up and go, but her body wanted to fuck, so she closed her eyes and let it happen. She let his fingers stroke her to her first orgasm.

After she ended up in his bed, she let another man penetrate her body for the first time since she laid eyes on Gregory. She let another man give her orgasm after orgasm, and by the time they were done, she knew she couldn't go home.

Chapter Sixteen

Janiece

"Can you believe that they are kicking me out of my house? I am like, who in the fuck are these people? Because they were surely different before my husband died. And they want a DNA test. Are you fucking kidding me? They know damn well that this is Isaiah's child. I lost my husband, and I'm going to be a damn single mom raising a child who will never know who her father was, and they are doing this bullshit to me," Janiece cried, pacing.

"I cheated on Greg," Janelle said, and Janiece didn't hear her clearly because she said it so softly.

"Then get this, this bitch Iyeshia gon' make me slap the shit outta her. If I wasn't eight months pregnant, wait! Hold up, what in the fuck did you just say?" she said, realizing that the look on Janelle's face wasn't good. She heard her mumble something, but that look of terror needed to be addressed.

"I cheated on Gregory," she repeated.

"Oh, my Lord," Janiece said and grabbed her stomach with her other hand. The baby heard the horrible announcement too, because she started to kick hard. "Nellie, please say you're lying. Cheated how? Like a date, a kiss, dinner? Define fucking 'cheated,'" Janiece yelled. "What in the hell did you exactly do, Janelle?"

"I slept with Devon," she answered with tear-filled eyes.

Janiece looked at her like she was insane. "Who in the fuck is Devon?" she yelled in disbelief.

"A man I met a few weeks ago. I've been seeing him, Janiece," she confessed.

Janiece then slid down onto the sofa that she was standing next to. "Oh, Nellie, why did you do that? And why did you not tell me that you were creeping or even met someone else?"

"You were at K.P.'s with your own issues, Jai, and I was too ashamed," she said, putting her head down.

"Well, you ought to be," she spat.

"Jai, are you serious right now? You were K.P.'s side piece for years," she shot.

"And I was wrong as fuck, and you made me feel like the worst person every chance you got, so yes, I am serious right now!" she snapped back.

"Don't yell at me. I feel horrible enough," she cried.

"As you should, and you must shut it all down. You are a mother. You have a family. If Greg finds out, you will break his heart, and your marriage will end."

"I know, and everything you say is true, but I like him, sissy. I don't know if I want to stop seeing him."

Janiece looked at her big sister for the first time with disappointment and wanted to slap her face. "Please tell me I didn't hear what I think I heard come out of your damn mouth."

"It's true."

"Nellie, you gave me so much grief when I fucked around with K.P., and now you go and have a damn affair. You must walk away now before it turns into something more," she said, and Janelle nodded. Janiece had a strong feeling that she hadn't convinced Janelle to do the right thing, but she was grown, had her own problems going on, and her baby was growing out of control, so she was quiet.

"It's worse," Janelle said, and Janiece's head lifted.

"Oh, my Lord, what could be worse than having an affair, Nellie?"

"He doesn't know that I am married with two kids. I lied," she confessed.

"Oh, my God, Janelle," she yelled.

"I know, Jai. I was upset with Greg when I met him, and I lied, okay? Now I'm terrified to tell him."

"You gotta be kidding me. You sound just like K.P. right now. You must stop and tell him, Nellie, sooner rather than later. You are playing with someone's heart, so you have to walk away, just block him and not talk to him anymore if you don't have the courage to come clean. What you are doing is cruel and selfish as fuck."

"Jai, I want to tell him, but how? Now that we have slept together, it's more complicated."

"How is it so damn complicated, Janelle?"

"Because he is so amazing. I can't think of anything else but him. Greg and I have fucked maybe five times since the twins were born. I met Devon, and he is smart, intelligent, an awesome cook, fine as fuck, and he fucked me better than Gregory has ever fucked me in the entire time that we've been together, and now I'm going out of my mind because I just want him. I love Greg and my kids, but I crave Devon."

"Janelle, listen to me. All affairs are fun, fucked filled, and all that jazz, but you have a whole husband, sissy. Do you really and truly want to give that up? Fuck all this 'new and igniting my flame' bullshit and fix your marriage while you still can."

"I don't know how. I believe that Greg is out there screwing bitches on me," she spat.

"Then divorce his ass. Janelle, we've been through this. You have no proof that he is having an affair. Even if he is, that is not a ticket to ride another man's dick. Listen to me, big sis. Go to Devon and shut that shit down. Work at or at least dissolve your marriage. If you don't, people will be hurt, and you don't want that. I've been through it, and it's not entertaining."

"Okay, okay, all right, sissy. I will," she said.

Janiece eyed her sister and knew she was lying, but she let it go. She had to learn, and Janiece decided to worry about her own problems.

Janelle assured Janiece that she would end things with Devon, but as soon as he called her on her way home, she rerouted her trip and went to him. As bad as she hated to admit it, she liked him a lot. She then related to K.P., something she never thought she'd do because she had no idea back then what it was like to be in a failing marriage. She called Gregory and lied to him again. She blamed it all on her grieving sister and how bad she needed her to stay, and her husband was so understanding. Those small moments of appreciating him for being so great when she was lying to him made her feel like shit, but not shitty enough to not go to Devon's.

She got to his place, and after they fucked, Devon started in with the questions she didn't want to answer, like where she lived and worked. She wished she could tell him the truth.

"Baby, please let me sleep. I told you my sister has been staying with me. She lost her husband, and I've just been working and being there for her. She is pregnant, and it's only been a short time since Isaiah died. Please believe me, things will be different soon. She most likely will move back home after the baby is born. I just don't want to entertain at my place until my sister is gone," she lied again.

She then went for his dick. If they were fucking, there were no questions. That night she stayed over all night. She woke up the next morning in a panic and was glad he was in the shower. She grabbed her phone and went into the living room to call Greg. She lied to him again and told him she was leaving Janiece's. Greg was good and didn't give her any grief, and after she hung up, Devon cleared his throat, and she turned to him. "Good morning."

"Good morning. Is everything good?"

"Yeah, I just had to call and check on Janiece. I wanted to let her know that I'd be there soon."

"Okay, do you want breakfast?" he said, heading into the kitchen. He wore a towel low on his waist, and she wanted him for breakfast.

"No, babe, I'm good. I'm going to dress and head out."

"Okay, well, I'm going to at least make coffee," he offered.

She nodded and headed into his master. She had to pee, so she made a mad dash to relieve herself and then quickly dressed. She walked out, and he gave her a to-go cup of coffee. "Thanks so much, Devon. You are so perfect."

"You are too, and I'm so glad we met, Janelle, but I won't lie. I feel like you are holding back or hiding something."

"Really? Why? Because you've never been to my house? Trust me, I don't live in my car, and I just need you to be patient. My li'l sister is going through it."

"You are so put together. I know you don't live in your car, but at least what do you do? I mean, your handbag and shoes cost more than somebody's rent. I am just so open, and you seem so secretive, babe, and I want to get to *know you* know you. I'm feeling you," he expressed.

"I've been hurt and brokenhearted, Devon, so this is my pace. Please know that I am feeling you too, babe, and this is good to me."

He smiled and then kissed her lips. "Can I see you tonight? I can come over and cook for you and your sister," he offered, and she almost choked on her coffee.

She coughed until she could clear her pipe. "Babe, that sounds good, but I don't want to be all up in her face with my new boo when her man just died. I'll come by later, though," she said and went up on her toes to kiss him.

"Okay, tonight I'll just order in then."

"Sounds good. Now I must go," she said and hurried her ass out of his place. She got in her car and got herself mentally together before heading home.

When she got there, the house was empty. Greg left a note on the island saying he took the twins to day care and headed to work for an early meeting. She rushed up to wash the night of passion with Devon off her skin. She then put on some loungewear and decided not to even power on her computer. She spent her day drinking, crying, and trying to figure out what she was going to do.

Chapter Seventeen

Janiece

She sat waiting for the nurse to call her name at what she hoped was her last doctor's appointment, because her due date was super close. Finally, the nurse called her back. It took her a couple of extra minutes to get up. She blew out a deep breath on her feet and moved slowly in the direction of the door to the back offices. She waited a little longer for the doctor to finally examine her and was shocked that she was already two centimeters. This was her first pregnancy, so she truly didn't know what that meant, but she left knowing that her daughter could show up any day.

Everything was crazy because she was stressed. Isaiah's family was doing the most, harassing her about whether the baby was Isaiah's and if she had been cheating with K.P. the entire time. Iyeshia had told them the full story of it all, and they doubted that she even loved Isaiah at all. Her only peace was when she was at K.P.'s. He did everything he could to make her smile, and the kids did their best to make sure she was always laughing. If she wanted to cry, K.J. was her new go-to for laughs.

After her appointment, she got into her car and headed home. When she pulled up, she saw a sheriff's car in front of her place, and she wondered what was up. She pulled into her driveway and saw the uniformed officer talking to her sister-in-law, and she said, "What now?"

She parked and hurried out to see what was happening and why the sheriff was at her home. She was over Isaiah's family and their antics, and the fact that she hadn't gotten a dime of Isaiah's insurance had her going out of her mind. The money she had gotten from the other policy was fine, but it wouldn't last long with the debt she had already spent. Eventually, she knew she had to go back to work, but being pregnant, work was the last thing on her mind.

"Iyeshia, what's going on?" Janiece questioned, holding her stomach. She noticed that the baby would move more when she got upset or frazzled. She was tired and not in the mood for any drama that afternoon. She just wanted to relax.

"Well, I'm glad you are here," she said with a smirk. "This is a notice of eviction. You have thirty days to be out of my brother's house," she announced with a look of pleasure.

Janiece took the notice and took a couple of steps back, wishing she could lean against something. "What! What do you mean 'eviction,' Iyeshia? You can't be serious. Where am I supposed to go in thirty short days? The baby is close to being due, Iyeshia. Y'all can't do this."

"That's your problem," she shot and started to walk away.

"Iyeshia, why are y'all doing this to me? You know thirty days is not enough time to move. My condo is leased. I can't do this right now. I am overwhelmed as it is. My husband died, and I am pregnant, and I . . . I . . ." she stuttered. "Do y'all even care about this baby? She is Isaiah's."

"So you say, and until we know the truth, no, we don't give a shit. This kid you claim is my brother's will be tested, and trust that every dime we have from him will be for the baby if she is my brother's kid," she said with "fuck you, Janiece" written all over her face.

Janiece just swiped at her tears and hurried inside. She took a seat on the steps and cried. She wished she could have a drink, but she just sat and sobbed. After a while, she dug her phone from her purse and called K.P.

"What the fuck?" he asked after she told him what had happened.

"Yes, that is what is happening. I don't know why they are doing this to me. I love my husband, and I hate that he died, and I can't comprehend why they just turned on me like this."

"Listen, you are okay, and don't worry. I will get the best lawyers for you, and you can fight them, Janiece. They are not going to just screw you out of everything."

"I can't afford lawyers, K.P. I have a child coming, and I paid off a lot of debt thinking they'd cut me a check. They haven't given me a dime. I have less than twenty thousand dollars left, and I don't have a job, K.P. I have a baby coming who is going to be gone in the blink of an eye."

"Janiece, baby, listen to me. I got you, and fuck that house. I'll buy you a new one. You are not going to be bullied by these people. I am here for whatever you need. Pack a bag. I'll be there soon, and we will figure it out. You don't have to beg them for shit. I got you and the baby, so fuck them!"

"They gave me thirty days to be out," she returned.

"Thirty days too long. I'll have your shit packed and moved out by tomorrow. I have a six-bedroom house, and you and your baby are welcome until you get back on your feet. Go pack, and I'll be there soon," he insisted.

They ended the call, and she went and packed two huge suitcases. She had to have movers pack up her place, so she needed to go and get a few items that wouldn't go to storage.

She hated having to call K.P. and not reach out to Janelle. She had enough going on with her marriage, so she did not want to be an added burden to her sister.

As promised, K.P. took care of everything, and the Lawtons' house was empty within the next four days. She stored the furnishings and things she didn't need and took a small U-Haul of things she needed for her and the baby. She didn't talk to Isaiah's family again after the day she put the key in his father's hand.

She settled in at K.P.'s in a guest room that was another spacious master with an en suite bath, and being there with his kids kept her in a good mood. K.P. worked long hours, which was okay because she felt tired since the baby was close to being due. She was sleeping if she wasn't laughing with the kids or eating. K.P. insisted that she use a spare room to set up for the baby, and after a week of him pushing, she agreed. He didn't hold back on the spending. Each day, something new arrived, and within a week, there was a nursery.

Just a week before her due date, she woke up to sharp back pains. She got up and went to the bathroom, and when she wiped, the tissue was pink. That was not normal, so she flushed, washed her hands, and tried to rest again. Another pain hit her, and she shot up. She stood, took deep breaths like she had learned, and decided to go and wake K.P. This was labor, she knew, because the pain was more intense. She paused again and leaned against the wall when another pain hit, and she knew this was it. She tapped on his door and then pushed it open without him inviting her in.

"Kerry," she said, and he jumped out of his sleep.

"Yeah, yeah, yes," he said, startled.

"I think I'm in labor," she said.

"Are you sure?"

"I really don't know. I'm just having pain. I've never been in labor before, so I don't know. I'm just definitely feeling a different pain."

"Do you want to go to the hospital?" he asked.

She stood there a moment or two and thought she might be okay when she didn't feel anything. "Maybe it's still a bit too early. I'm sorry to wake you."

"No, don't be sorry, and are you sure you're good?"

She stood there a few more moments to see if the pain would return, and when it didn't, she nodded. "I think I'm okay, but can I lie here with you? I'm nervous, K.P."

"Sure, of course," he said and pulled back the covers. He moved over to the other side, and she got in.

She got in, and they settled in, and five minutes later, another pain hit her, and she moaned.

"Jai, are you okay?"

"No, no, no," she said, breathing through another contraction.

He got up and turned on the lamp. "We should get you to the hospital, just to make sure."

"No, K.P., you have work in the morning. I don't want to," she tried to say and then groaned in pain.

"Nonsense. We are going to the hospital."

She sat up and agreed. She watched him dress quickly while she sat beside his bed. "The kids? What about the kids?"

"Phyllis is here. The kids are asleep and will be fine. I'll let her know. Now stand up so I can get you to the car."

She grabbed his outstretched hands, and he pulled her up. Another pain hit her, and that time she didn't moan, but she let out a sound of discomfort. "Are you okay?" he asked.

"No, no, no," she said, shaking her head. "It hurts, K.P. This shit really hurts," she expressed between breaths.

"Come on, baby, let me get you to the car, and then I'll get the baby bag," he said.

She nodded and allowed him to help her.

After what seemed like hours to Janiece, she was finally at the hospital. Then it would be time to get the baby out. She was on four centimeters but in a lot of pain. She demanded an epidural, and not long after, she wasn't crying in pain. Four hours later, she had given birth to her baby girl, and she was exhausted but happier than any day she could remember.

K.P. was by her side for the entire delivery, and he was the one to cut the baby's cord. She confirmed that it was okay for K.P. to go to the nursery while they cleaned her up and bathed the baby. When they returned to her room, Janiece was more than anxious to hold her little girl. She was a tiny replica of Isaiah, and Janiece was grateful that God gave her an image to remind her of Isaiah. She admired her bundle and then let her latch on to nurse.

"Marry me," K.P. blurted, and she looked at him.

"What?"

"Marry me, Jai. I love you and want you and this little girl to be with me," he said.

She was shocked and speechless, but she saw the love and sincerity in his eyes. She knew her answer wasn't thought-out, and the drugs may not have completely worn off when she said, "Yes." She smiled. "Yes, I will."

Chapter Eighteen

Janiece

Janiece nursed her angel and awaited the visit of Isaiah's family. She asked K.P. to leave because she wanted to keep the peace and did not want any family feuds at the hospital. After burping the little one, she was leaning over to put her in the hospital's bassinet when the door opened after a soft tap. It was Isaiah's mom, and Janiece was happy to see her.

"Mom, hey, come on in. I was just putting her down," she said, smiling.

"Oh, my goodness, I have my first grandbaby," she gushed, coming in closer. "How are you, Janiece? How was your labor, dear?"

"It was hard, but I did it. I wish Isaiah had been by my side, but . . ." she said and then paused. "I did it, and there she is. I am tired, but I'm good."

She smiled and touched her hand. "Good, good."

"Where is the firing squad? I was sure your hubby and daughter would come in to ruin the happiest moment I've had since my husband died," she said and looked down at her hands.

"I'm alone," she answered. She looked over at the baby and then back at Janiece. "Isaac and Iyeshia are so close and just alike. Their crazy theory of this not being my son's daughter is not mine, so they didn't want to come."

"I guess that was best," Janiece said sadly.

She took Janiece's hand. "I'm sorry and can't speak for them, but I am here to meet my granddaughter."

"Well, thank you for coming, and you can pick her up if you'd like."

Isaiah's mom put her jacket and purse on the window ledge and went into the bathroom. Janiece heard the water and knew she was washing her hands. She came back, took her bundle from the bassinet, and gazed at her.

"She is so beautiful, and she looks like Iyeshia. If they see her, they will know that she is a Lawton."

"Yeah, a female version of Isaiah equals Iyeshia. She does look like her aunt."

"She does," she added and then took a seat. "I want you to know that I am not on board with my daughter and husband. I knew my son was a very intelligent man. I know how much he loved and adored you, Janiece. They are taking his death so hard, their judgment is so clouded, and they are taking their anger out on you because they need to find some way to express or release shit, I don't know. When I heard the news that my child, my son, my only son died, my heart just . . ." she said, and tears fell. She swiped at them. "I just want to be a part of my granddaughter's life. She is a part of him, and I am tired of trying to reason with Isaac and Iyeshia, and I am tired of trying to convince them to not do the DNA test because now that she is here, her little face is the answer to all of the unanswered questions they have.

"I have pressed and pressed for Isaac to cut you the check and not remove you from the house. Don't think I'm not on your side. I just can't understand why they are so bitter toward you, and I am sorry. I know this is my grandchild, and I want a relationship with you and my grandbaby. Please let me have that," she asked.

Janiece smiled. "Of course, Mom. I'd never deny your family access to Isaiah's daughter. She is a Lawton. Despite what your daughter thinks, I've never cheated on my husband," she said, and a tear fell.

"Look, please, don't feel like you have to explain. I don't care to know the details of how you and my son started or anything about that other man. I met you, and my son married you. That is all I see. If you have moved on or even if you are with him, that is your decision and your business. My son died, and you can decide when you want to move on. You don't owe a damn person an explanation for what you want."

Janiece smiled. "I know Iyeshia embellished the relationship that K.P. and I had, and I'll be honest, until my baby was born, everything with us was platonic, and he asked me to marry him today, and I said yes. K.P. has been here for me every day, and I said yes. I still love Isaiah, but I am alive. I want love and happiness, and I honestly don't know if I'm moving too fast or not fast enough. I know I'm here with this beautiful baby girl, and I am broke because I was put out of my home and didn't get any of my husband's insurance money, so right now, I must make a way and life for myself and my daughter.

"I chose Isaiah. I didn't choose K.P., but right now, he is all I got, and I will fall back in love with him because he is the only man I've loved other than Isaiah. K.P. is patient, and he has helped me make it through the worst moment of my life. I lost my husband and my home, and I spent a lot of money believing that I'd get my husband's insurance money, so the way things went down like pushed me back to him. My love for Isaiah didn't die like he did." She began to sob. Isaiah's mom stood, put the baby down, and then consoled Janiece.

"I understand more than you know, and I just want you happy. Regarding the insurance, just give them the DNA test, so you can get your money and move on. I want to show them they misjudged you, so please, let's just do the damn test so we can move on, and my granddaughter will always be a part of my life even if neither of them accept her."

"Isaiah has to be smiling in heaven to hear you say that. Jaiden is a lucky little girl to have a grandma like you."

"You named her Jaiden?"

"No, Isaiah did months ago."

"Well, it suits her precious little self. She is so adorable, and this DNA shit is nonsense. She is a replica of the twins when they were born," she said, picking up the baby again.

She spent another couple of hours with them before she kissed both goodbye. She assured Janiece that she would come by K.P.'s if that was what it took to see her grandbaby. Janiece was fine with that since Doreen was the only one interested in knowing her grandchild. Plus, she was relieved that she didn't feel like her father and sister-in-law about her.

As soon as Doreen left, she called K.P. to let him know that she was gone and that things had gone far better than she thought they would. After about forty-five minutes, K.P. walked in with a giant teddy bear and a bag from one of Janiece's favorite eateries. She smiled and shook her head at the insanely large teddy bear.

"K.P., really, that big-ass pink bear shared a ride to the hospital with you?"

"No, I got it from the gift shop, and I couldn't resist."

"How are we going to get home with that giant-ass bear?" she asked, and he placed it on the window seat.

"I'll make it happen, trust me." He smiled and went over to her hospital bed. He placed the bag in front of her, and she grabbed it quickly.

"You didn't," she said, opening the bag.

"I did. You did an amazing job delivering this little girl, and you deserve it," he said and then gave her a quick kiss.

"I'm about to devour this sandwich," she said, removing items from the bag. K.P. announced that he had food in that bag also. He took a moment to look at the baby and then sat in the chair. Then her door opened again, and it was her sister.

"I'm an auntie," she said, walking in excitedly. She rushed over to kiss and hug her sister. "And you are now a mommy," she said, taking off her coat and putting it on the coatrack. She did the same with her purse and went into the bathroom. Janiece heard the water and guessed she was washing her hands.

"Yes, I'm a mommy, and you missed the entire thing. You were supposed to be with me during my labor, and you ignored my calls," Janiece announced a bit louder to talk over the running water.

Janelle walked out of the bathroom, dried her hands, then tossed the paper towel into the can near the door. She went over to the bassinet and picked up the baby. "I'm sorry, sis, and I'll explain later, okay?"

Janiece said nothing. She just went back to unpacking her food.

"Oh, my goodness, Jai, she is so gorgeous and looks a lot like Isaiah."

"Thank you," she said, and K.P. stood.

"Hey, Janelle," he said.

"K.P.," she said, turning in his direction. "I didn't know you were here," she said, and Janiece figured she paid no attention to him sitting by the window in the chair. "Hey, what's going on?"

"Nothing much, and how about you? How is Greg?"

"We're fine," she said with her eyes on the baby.

"We should get together soon after Janiece comes home."

"K.P. asked me to marry him, and I said yes," Janiece said, jumping in.

"No way! A baby and a new husband. This is better than the Michael Jordan comeback," she joked, and Janiece laughed, wondering why that never got old for her.

"Yes, I guess it is," she said, and K.P. leaned in and kissed Janiece.

"What happened with the Lawtons? Did they see this little girl and drop their silly idea of this not being Isaiah's child?"

Janiece was done opening the wrapper on her sandwich and took her first bite and moaned as she chewed. She swallowed and then answered her sister's question. "They have no plans of backing off, sis. They still want the test."

"That's fucked up, and you better save me a piece of that Italian beef," she said, taking a seat at the foot of Janiece's bed.

"Whatever, girl."

"And what about the house? Are they seriously not letting you and their granddaughter move back in?"

"I didn't ask about the house," she said after swallowing her food.

"And she doesn't need that house. We have a house," K.P. added before taking a seat in the chair. Janiece smiled at him.

"True," Janelle said, continuing to admire her niece. "She is so adorable. Hey, li'l Jai. Hey, li'l Jai. Now we got us a li'l Jai," she said, and Janiece stopped chewing.

Her words hit her, and she remembered Isaiah saying he wanted his big Jai and li'l Jai. That made her feel so horrible. She knew she was moving on too fast.

She put her sandwich down and then grabbed the baby's blanket that sat near her on her hospital bed and covered her face. She began to sob, and she felt a touch on her arm. She knew it was him. She knew his touch.

"Jai, babe, what's wrong?" he inquired, and she cried even harder.

"Janiece, what's wrong, sis?" she asked.

She cried for a few more moments and then removed the blanket. "I can't. I can't marry you, K.P. I'm sorry, but it's too soon, and I can't. I'm not ready," she said through sobs. The only sounds after that were the sobs of Janiece and her now-crying infant.

Chapter Nineteen

Janiece

Janiece unloaded the last of her things from Janelle's car. Janiece now lived with her sister and her family. Going back to K.P.'s never happened, and she hated that she had to stay with her sister, but she had no other options, and it was best because being at K.P.'s would have been too much. She didn't even allow him to get her and the baby from the hospital. It had been five weeks, and she was miserable. She missed him and Isaiah, and she hated being alone to raise her daughter. She was sad all the time and cried too much. She loved her husband, but she was now back in love with K.P. She hated that she wanted to just run back to him.

She awoke to the sound of her ringing phone. The ID read K.P., and then she hit ignore. He had been calling and texting, and she continued to ignore him. She knew he loved her, but she just wasn't ready.

"Hey, sis, you wanna talk about it?" she heard Janelle's voice from behind.

"I just wish he were still here. I wish he hadn't died and left us alone," she answered.

Janelle came all the way into the room. She grabbed her sister's hand, and they sat on the bed. "I know, Jai, and I can't imagine how difficult it is, but I know you will be okay eventually."

"I mean, I know he's gone, but it still seems like he is just over there defending this country, and he will be back. My husband's casket is in the ground empty. They didn't even bring his body home to me," she cried.

"Janiece, sissy, I am so sorry, but you can't keep doing this to yourself. You can't keep feeling guilty and denying any happiness for yourself. You have to get back to living and have a life. I've witnessed you letting the baby cry it out while you were zoned out. You have to stop. It's not healthy, Janiece. You didn't die, and there is nothing wrong with moving on. What happened to Isaiah was out of your control, and it is okay to love again. It is okay for you to smile and be happy," she said.

"I don't know how. I want him here. I want him to be here, and it's like I don't deserve to be happy after he died a horrible death over there," Janiece cried.

"I'm sorry he is gone, and you will have to accept it, sis, and move on. You can't be miserable for the rest of your life. Isaiah wouldn't even want that for you. Being in this miserable state won't bring him back or make you happy."

"Do you think he'd want me back with K.P.?" she asked.

"You want me to be honest?"

"Yes," she answered and swiped at a tear.

"If K.P. is the one to bring you happiness, he will. He loves you that much, so stop ignoring that man's calls and texts and let him love you. K.P. and you started out horribly, but that shit doesn't matter. It's how you end. If you love him, let him make you happy."

Janiece smiled a half-smile and then dried her eyes with a nod to what her sister had said. Janelle was right.

"He loves you, Janiece. I can see it in his eyes. When I went for the rest of your things, he looked defeated. You love him, so stop depriving yourself of happiness. Isaiah would want you to choose happiness and not wear the same pajamas for four damn days."

"I was so mean to him, Nellie, and I've ignored him. I was horrible to just leave him like that."

"It's better late than never, Jai. You need to go to him. K.P. will have you."

"You think so?"

"Yes. Do you love him? Be honest."

"Yes, I do," she admitted.

"Then get your funky ass up and go bathe, brush yo' damn teeth, do something with this hair, and put on whatever you can fit in that is cute and go get him," she encouraged her, and Janiece stood. Janelle stood and hugged her tight before making her exit.

Janiece went over to pick up her baby. "Well, Jaiden Marie, your momma is going to choose happiness today, and I pray that you understand. I loved your daddy, and he was everything to me. I love him still, but I love Kerry, too, and he is here, and I wanna be happy again. Please don't ever be mad at me for remarrying."

Her baby smiled at her, and Janiece smiled back, seeing her husband's face all over hers. "You're smiling just like your daddy. You have your daddy's smile, little one," she cooed. "Yes, you do, li'l momma. Yes, you do." She planted kisses on her baby's face and then put her down so she could get herself together. She was going to get her man.

Chapter Twenty

K.P.

He was resting on the sofa, half watching the television, when the doorbell rang. He sat up and wondered who would come by his place without notice at that hour. He rarely ever had guests, and he especially didn't entertain uninvited guests. He put the remote down and thought maybe it was Kimberly. She'd be the only one to come by without a heads-up. When he opened the door, he was shocked to see Janiece.

"Jai?" he asked with his head tilted to the side.

"Hey, Kerry, I'm sorry for just showing up so late and without calling," she said, rubbing her hands together. K.P. knew her. It was a sign that she was nervous about something.

"No, it's okay. Come in," he said, letting her step inside. He closed the door, and he offered to take her coat. She took it off and put her purse on the front entrance bench. "Is everything okay?" he asked, going over to the coat closet.

"Yeah, everything is fine. Everyone is fine."

"Okay, that is good to know. Can I get you anything?"

"Merlot is good," she answered.

"Wine? Did you stop nursing?"

"No, but I'm pumped, and I need wine, please."

"Sure, go on in the living room and have a seat, and I'll be there in a moment."

He entered the kitchen, grabbed a bottle of red from the wine rack, and opened it. He grabbed a glass from the cabinet, poured her half a glass, and then went ahead and poured more. Janiece never did five-ounce pours. She was a nine-ounce-pour woman. He walked over to the sofa, where she sat, and handed her the glass. Before he could take a seat, she had the glass up to her lips. He grabbed the remote and muted the television. She set her glass down on the coffee table with most of the contents already gone.

"Is everything okay? How is the baby?"

"Everything is good, and Jaiden is fine with her little fat self."

"Wow. I'd love to see her," he expressed, and then she grabbed her glass and polished it off. She handed it to him, and he knew that was his cue to fix her another. Whatever she had come to say to him had to be bad, he thought as he stood.

After he refilled her glass and gave it to her, he went for his liquor cart and poured himself a double shot of Johnnie Walker Blue. He sat, and they were both quiet and just sipped. "So what is it? Did you come to tell me some bad news?"

She shook her head and took another swallow before returning the glass to the coffee table.

"I came here to tell you I'm sorry," she said.

"No, I'm the one who's sorry," he tried to say, but she cut him off.

"No, wait," she said, lifting her hand to pause his words. "Please just let me say what I have to say."

He gave a head gesture for her to continue.

"First, I'm sorry for leaving the hospital without telling you and ignoring your million attempts to talk to me."

"Jai, it's—" he tried to interrupt again.

"No, please allow me to finish," she stressed, putting a hand on top of his.

"Okay, continue."

"I'm sorry, babe, and I'm ready," she said, looking him in his eyes. "I know you love me, and I know that you are good for Jaiden and me, and I am here because I love you too. I am ready for you to love, spoil, and take care of me, and to give Jaiden and me a family with you and the kids. I was foolish to think I didn't deserve to start over and have a happy life because I lost Isaiah. I don't feel like that anymore, and I don't want to be alone or without you anymore. Losing Isaiah was so horrible, and it was hard for me to let go of the idea that I was being a horrible person to run back to you of all people. I can't bring him back. Even if I stayed away from you for one hundred years, it wouldn't bring him back to me. You made me happy, and I want to be happy again," she said, and the tears that brimmed her eyes finally fell.

He looked at her for a few moments before he spoke. "Are you sure? Because my heart can't take you walking out on me again," he said, hoping that this meant they'd finally be together.

"I'm more than sure," she said and leaned in to kiss him. He didn't pull away. He just closed his eyes and let his lips linger on hers for a few moments.

He pulled back. "Do you really mean what you are saying to me?"

"Yes, and I'd like to marry you if you still want to marry me," she announced, and his hand went to his chest.

He couldn't believe his ears. This had to be a dream, and he hoped that he didn't wake up from it. He just pulled her in and held her. He was overjoyed and over-whelmed at the same time, wondering what brought about this change, but he didn't dare ruin the moment with those types of questions. He just silently thanked God for bringing her back to him, and then he remembered the ring he had gotten for her. He had planned to give it to her the same night he returned with the big-ass bear that was still in the room that used to be Jaiden's nursery.

"Hold on, I have something for you," he said and got up. He went to his master and returned to Janiece sitting on the couch. "I wanted to give you this that night when I came back to the hospital, but the meltdown happened and . . ." he said, deciding not to rehash that. "Anyway, I would like to give you this and ask you again to be my wife."

"Of course," she said with a smile. He opened the box, and a look of confusion hit Janiece's face.

"What's wrong? You don't like it?"

"No, I love it, but I assumed it would be the ring you gave me before."

"Well, it's not."

"What did you do with it?"

"I used it as partial payment for this one if you must know. My jeweler is a good guy," he joked with a smile. "Can I?" he said, holding it up to offer it to her finger.

She held up her hand and let him slide the ring on and then let him slide inside her body. It didn't take long before they were under his sheets, reuniting and reconnecting. After two good sessions of heat, they were on the sofa in K.P.'s bedroom in front of the fire, wrapped in a cashmere blanket. Her body and the fabric felt so good to K.P.'s skin, and he didn't want to be anywhere else at that moment.

"What are you thinking about?" he asked her.

"Nothing and everything. I have a lot to do, and we have a lot to do."

"Like?"

"Moving and getting settled in all over again and talking to the kids, just a lot, and we are going to be busy for the next few weeks."

"Well, the transition will be smoother than you think. I'll hire someone to help you. Right now, just focus on the essentials. You can shop and get anything you need, and eventually, we will figure out your storage and shit. For now, no worries."

"Thanks, and can I ask you for one more thing?"

"Anything, sweetheart," he said and kissed the side of her head.

"If you see me crying or if I need some space, can you allow that without questions? I'm still mourning him even now when I am telling myself that this, us, is okay."

"I will, babe. I will give you whatever you need."

"Thanks," she said and turned around to kiss his lips.

"Anything, and you know what we should do?"

"What?" she asked, intrigued.

"We should just go to Vegas and do it. I mean, we've been together for a long time, and we don't have to have a long engagement," he suggested.

"Are you serious?"

"Dead serious. We know each other, and it would be so exciting."

"It would be. And you can finally meet my mom and my family, and we can finally have a normal and happy life."

"Yes. Where is your mom again?"

"Newport Beach, California."

"We could fly there, then go to Vegas and come back married."

"Wow, this is really happening, and we will finally be husband and wife. Kimberly is going to die," she laughed.

"She'll be cool. She is married, and the past is in the past, right?"

"That's right," she said and rested her head on his chest. They talked more, laughed even more, and he stroked her again before they finally fell asleep.

Chapter Twenty-one

Janiece

Her eyes fluttered when the light behind her lids was too bright to ignore. The smell of K.P.'s favorite cologne danced around her nose, but she still struggled to open her eyes. Finally, as she looked up at the ceiling, everything came back to her, and she wasn't at Janelle's in her guest room. She was at K.P.'s, and when she lifted her left hand, she saw the rock that he had slid on her finger the night before. She smiled. It was real, it wasn't a dream, and she sat up. She turned, and her legs dangled over the side of his bed.

"Good morning, beautiful," she heard from behind, so she turned in his direction, shocked to see he was fully dressed in a suit without his jacket.

"Good morning. You're already dressed for work?"

"I am, but I won't be at the office long. I have a few meetings this morning that I could not reschedule, so I'll be home early this afternoon," he said and leaned in to kiss her forehead.

"Okay, I must dress and get to Janelle's. I have never slept away from my baby, which is why I slept late."

"It's still early, just a little after seven. So grab my robe, go have some breakfast first, and there is a toothbrush and fresh towels on the vanity for you."

"Thanks, baby," she said, and he exited the room. She went into the bathroom, relieved her bladder, and washed her hands. She washed her hands and face and then brushed her teeth. She decided to take a quick shower, and after she dried her skin, she grabbed the robe from the back of the bathroom door and made sure she secured it because she had nothing on underneath it. She looked in the mirror, and a smile crept on her face. And she said out loud that it was okay to be happy. Then she headed for the kitchen.

"Janiece," K.J. yelled and ran to hug her. "I didn't know you were here," he said, and she hugged him back.

"Hey, li'l man. You were asleep last night when I got here," she said and kissed the top of his head. K.J. went back to his seat, and she turned to Kayla.

"Hey, Kayla," she spoke, and Kayla gave her a dry, barely audible, "Hey," before rolling her eyes. Janiece knew she still hated her, so she was satisfied that she'd even responded.

"Hey, Ms. Phyllis, what's on the menu? I can help if you need me," she said, going for her purse. She had to call Janelle because things moved so fast the night before, she hadn't called her.

"Ask Mr. King K.J.," she said, pulling things from the fridge. "So far, we have hotcakes, eggs, grits, and turkey sausage, but I know he'll want French toast before I'm done. That little boy swears that this is Restaurant Phyllis," she joked.

"Well, I plan to devour anything you make because I am hungry."

"Worked up an appetite last night, huh?" she said and gave Janiece a wink.

Janiece giggled and then headed to the living room to talk to Janelle.

"Hey, sissy," Janelle answered groggily.

"Hey, how is my sweet pea?"

"Terrible, girl. This li'l girl hates the bottle, Jai. She fussed with me for so long and wouldn't take the bottle, but when Greg took over, she took it. I think yo' baby got eyes for my husband," she joked.

"Awww, I'm sorry, sis. As soon as I am done with breakfast, I'm there. And I can't wait to tell you about last night and show you my ring. It's gorgeous," she said and heard someone suck their teeth. She looked up to see Kayla. She gave her a good eye roll and then rushed off.

She finished up her conversation with Janelle and went to look for Kayla. When she didn't find her in her room, she went to the room that was supposed to be Jaiden's nursery because that was the only door not closed. She pushed it open to find Kayla on the floor reclined on the oversized pink bear that K.P. had gotten for Jaiden.

The room had been dismantled some but still looked like it was a nursery in progress. "Can we talk?"

"About?"

"Us and why you don't like me?"

"Why does it matter if I like you? My dad likes you, so that should be enough," she spat.

Janiece wanted to join her on the floor, but she didn't want her robe to malfunction, so she pulled over the rocking chair and took a seat. "Well, Kayla, it does matter to me. Your dad and I are in love, and we are going to be married, and then we will be a family. I just want to know why you don't like me, so we can try to get past it," she said, looking at Kimberly's little twin. She looked so much like her, and Janiece hoped she'd grow up to be a better person than her mom and her.

"It doesn't matter," she said again, not looking up from her textbook.

"Kayla, honestly, it does, and I don't want us to be enemies."

"You stole my father's heart from my mom, and then he wanted you and your little girl, and you left him, so that is why I don't like you," she finally admitted, and her eyes watered.

Janiece thought she'd say, "Because you're a bitch," or some evil kid response, but she didn't expect that.

"Wow, kiddo, I can understand why you hate me so much, but I assure you, Kayla, it didn't go that way, not exactly," she said and took a deep breath. She had to tell her something that didn't glorify her role because she was dead wrong, and she knew it. "First, I want to say I am sorry for everything I did to you and your mom back then. Your father and I foolishly did something that we both knew was wrong, but we did it anyway, and I'm not proud of it, Kayla. Being with your dad before he ended things with your mom was so bogus, and I am sorry. My behavior was horrible. I never wanted to hurt you or your brother. I was just mixed up in some grown folks' misconduct.

"I know what I did was wrong, and I hope you can forgive me and give me another chance. Your dad means so much to me, and he loves me, Kayla. How we started was bad, I can definitely own up to that, but we are here now, and we love each other, Kayla. I am sorry I hurt you," Janiece said and sighed. "Then I left because I was going through a lot. My daughter's father died, and I was conflicted and confused about what was appropriate or not appropriate and needed space to think. After I took some time to process it all, I realized your dad was who I needed and wanted, and I had to get myself together so I could be good for him. I wasn't good for him before I took that time. Can you please forgive me and give me a chance? I love your dad, and all we want now is to be happy. I love you and your brother because I love your father so much and want us to get along."

Kayla looked around the room. It took her a few moments to process what Janiece said, and she saw her relax her shoulders. "So you're really here to stay this time? No more confusing stuff? You won't leave him again?"

"I will never leave him again. I love him, Kayla, and he is my family. You and K.J. are my family, and I want us all to be okay."

"I'll forgive you, but please don't hurt my father again. My dad was so sad when you didn't come to Vegas with us. Then he was so happy that you and your baby would come back here with us, but when we went to get you with flowers and balloons, you were gone, and later that night, when K.J. was asleep, I went downstairs for water, and my dad was on the couch crying. I have never heard my father cry, Ms. Janiece, but I knew he was crying because you and your baby didn't return to our house. He was different every day, and now he was finally back to his old self. You can't come and hurt him again. If you do, I will hate you for hurting my daddy again."

"Again, Kayla, I'm sorry, and I am here now, and I'm not leaving him ever again. I won't break his heart. Please believe that things are going to be good for us, and I hope we can get along."

"You have to promise," she said, and the look in her eyes meant that she was serious.

"I promise." She smiled at her.

Kayla put her eyes back on her book. Janiece stood, hoping they were okay, and then headed back to the kitchen.

The food smelled amazing, so she made a mimosa. Phyllis said it would be five more minutes, so Janiece made her way to K.P.'s office. He was on the phone, and she saw he was busy, so she gave him a quick kiss on the top of his head and went back to the kitchen. She was happy to see that Kayla had returned to the table, and she took a seat. K.J. talked nonstop about this robot he was building with his classmate Jonah, and Janiece enjoyed his lively personality. Kayla laughed more at him, making Janiece feel like they were making progress because she normally tuned her and K.J. out as if no one were talking. Ms. Phyllis loaded the table with dishes of delectable breakfast items, and everyone began to serve themselves. Now Kayla was in the mix with conversation as they discussed movie choices for that evening.

"Okay, I'm off to work," K.P.'s voice interrupted them, and he made his way around the table, giving his family kisses. He ended with Janiece and gave her a few more kisses than the one he planted on each of the kids, and they both smiled at each other.

"Babe, what would you like for dinner?" she asked, and he paused at the door.

"Whatever Phyllis puts together, I guess," he replied.

"No, babe, I'm going to cook. This will be my and Jaiden's first official night home, so I want to cook for us."

"Well, you know all of my favorites, so make whatever you feel like, babe," he said and grabbed his keys from the dish by the door.

"Gotcha, and I love you," she said. It felt good to say it out loud to him again.

"I love you too." He smiled and winked. "And, kids, I love y'all, but if your rooms look anything like they look now when you get home, there will be problems, so handle that," he instructed. K.J. and Kayla mumbled something, but K.P. was already out the door.

They ate, and after Phyllis assured her that she needed no help, Janiece dressed and headed to Janelle's. When she walked in, she went straight for her bundle and gave her multiple kisses. She then noticed her sister was looking sexy as hell before noon.

"Finally you are here," Janelle said, going for her handbag and keys. "She just ate, and I'm running late," she said in a rush.

"Janelle, stop, sissy, and tell me what you are doing."

"What do you mean, sis?"

"Nellie, you work from home, and you don't think I've noticed that you are dressing up in the middle of the day and dipping out of here? Or that you're grinning on the phone like a teen? You take three-hour store trips to Target, so come on, Nellie. It's me, sis. You are still messing with Devon, aren't you?"

"Jai, you don't understand," she tried to say.

"Bullshit! I understand. I fuckin' over-stand, so tell me the damn truth!" Janiece demanded.

"Fuck! Yes! Fuckin' yes! I am still seeing him!"

"Janelle, sis, I told you a long time ago to shut it down," Janiece said, putting her baby down in her bassinet. "You are going to hurt him and Greg, and you may end up alone, and it's so not worth it!"

"You kill me with this shit. You are always team Greg. What about me, sis?" she yelled. "You keep warning me, when you are getting your happily ever after with the man you fell in love with. Devon is different."

"So get a damn divorce! Janelle, listen to me. You have to either fix it with Greg or leave. This two-timing bullshit will break hearts and affect your damn kids. You are living a dangerous life with this, and K.P. and I didn't get here because we did something so great. We are here because my damn husband died, and K.P. is the only man I've ever loved other than Isaiah, so stop comparing my affair to yours. This shit is going to blow up in your face," she warned.

"I have to meet Devon. I have to go," Janelle said and exited the house through her garage door.

"I'm packing up and leaving tonight," Janiece yelled, but she didn't reply.

She picked up her baby and talked to her for a few more minutes before she got to work. She packed up the few items she had at Janelle's house and loaded K.P.'s vehicle. She was close to leaving and realized she didn't have her baby's car seat. "Damn!" she said, realizing she had left it in her car. She was headed back inside to call K.P. to tell him her new dilemma, and her phone rang. She looked at the ID and cringed at Iyeshia's name. She didn't want to pick up, but she did. "Hello."

"Janiece, your trifling ass needs to be at Hazel Crest Medical Center on Woodlawn this Wednesday for the test."

"Are we seriously still doing this? You've seen my daughter. You know she is a Lawton."

"Well, the way we see it is you are a ho-ass liar. You didn't even tell anyone you were pregnant until weeks after Isaiah was gone, so yes, we are still doing this."

"We don't have any of Isaiah's DNA. How is any of this possible?" Janiece asked, confused.

"My father, you idiot," she spat.

"Fuck you!" Janiece yelled and then hung up. Then after Iyeshia's failed call attempts, she started to text.

Iyeshia: If you want a dime of his insurance, you will be there.

Jai: I will be there just to show you and your crazy-ass father the truth. I don't give a damn about the money!

Iyeshia: And we will want joint custody. You can't keep my brother's child from us.

Jai: I never tried to. Y'all are the ones who didn't want to see her. I've never denied any of you!

Iyeshia: Whatever, ho. We will be in touch, and make sure you are there so we can get this DNA shit over with.

Janiece didn't even reply to that. She called K.P. because she needed the car seat.

"Hey, you," he answered.

"Hey, do you have a quick second?"

"Yeah, what's up? I have a meeting in five, so what's going on?"

"They still want the test," she said.

"So give them the test. You did nothing wrong, so let 'em have it."

"I just hate that I have to do this shit for them. They are being fuckin' ridiculous, K.P."

"And that's more reason why you need to give it to them. Show them and give them the finger. If they want to give you your portion, they will, and if they don't, so fuckin' what? I gotta go, love."

"One more thing. I forgot Jaiden's car seat in my car."

"Okay, after this meeting, I'll run to Target, grab one, and I'll be there. There are no problems, babe, only solutions. I love you."

"I love you too." She smiled, and they ended the call.

She went back to loading the Hummer, and she managed to get all of her things in. She waited, and K.P. finally arrived with a brand-new car seat. She agreed that he should drive the loaded Hummer, and she and the baby rode in his car. When they made it, as promised, Phyllis had all the things she needed to cook for her family. Dinner went well with lots of laughter and jokes, and Phyllis refused to let her clean after they were done.

"After we are married, I want to adopt Jaiden and give her my last name," he said, and her head popped up from his lap.

"K.P., I don't know about that. Isaiah's family is already trying to prove that she is a Lawton. Adopting her and changing her name may not be a good idea."

"I hear you and understand that, but know I plan to be a good dad to her, too," he assured her.

"I know, and that is one of the reasons I love you. You and Kimberly had y'all's issues, but you didn't drop the ball with your kids."

He smiled. "They are my only successes from that marriage," he said.

"Yes, and I am happy to finally be a mom. It took a while to make her, so I'm grateful God left me with a part of him."

"I bet," he said, and she relaxed on his lap again.

"I'm happy," she said and then closed her eyes. He caressed her arm, and she quickly dozed off.

The monitor on the coffee table woke her, and she sat up. K.P. was sleeping with his head laid back. She went for her crying baby and woke her sleeping fiancé. By the time she got into bed with him, she was at ease. She was more relaxed than she had been since the day Isaiah got on that plane to leave, and she was settled that things would finally be okay.

Chapter Twenty-two

Janiece

Janiece sat waiting impatiently for her in-laws to show up. She bounced her baby on her knee when they filed into the waiting room. Doreen smiled, but Isaac and Iyeshia wore the same scowl, but Janiece stood to greet them. Doreen reached for her grandbaby and blessed her cheeks with grandmotherly kisses. The baby was all smiles and happy to see her grandmother. They all sat, and Doreen doted on her grandbaby.

"With that face, she looks just like Esha when she was a baby, and don't deny it, Isaac," she said, and he didn't even look at the baby. He stayed stone-faced.

"No, Mother, I can't see it," Iyeshia voiced, and Janiece wanted to just jump her ass.

"It's okay, Mom. They can pretend like they don't recognize the resemblance or not even look at her at all. This stupid test that y'all are insistent on doing is bogus."

"Young lady, I don't get two shits about looks."

"Un-fucking-believable!" Iyeshia spat.

"Iyeshia," Doreen said, "what is your problem now?"

"This bitch is rocking a big-ass diamond. This bitch come up in here with a rock larger than life. Hell, yes, we are testing this fuckin' kid."

"Her fuckin' name is Jaiden, Iyeshia, and I don't owe you or your family an explanation of how I spend the rest of my life. My life ain't yo' business. My daughter is a Lawton, and she is y'all only business with me. Mom, please take her back with y'all. I can't with your husband and your crazy-ass daughter," Janiece spat and then got up. She vacated the doctor's office and went outside.

Tears fell from her eyes as she tried to figure out how they had come to that moment. When Isaiah was alive and home, they treated her like she was a person. Now she was bitch this and bitch that. She just wanted to get the test over with. She didn't owe them shit. She had a right to live her life as she chose.

After what seemed like hours of Janiece pacing the waiting room, they finally brought the baby out, and Doreen handed her to Janiece. She planted several kisses on her baby before giving Doreen a hug goodbye. She promised to keep in touch, and she told Doreen that she could see and spend time with Jaiden as much as she wanted. She tried to apologize for Iyeshia and Isaac, but Janiece told her it wasn't her fault that they were treating her horribly.

She headed home and called K.P. She filled him in on that afternoon's events, and he assured her that all would be good. Before they ended the call, he told her Kim would be by that evening for the kids, and that instantly made her uncomfortable. She hadn't seen her in too long and had no idea how their meeting would go since Janiece technically took her man.

"Do you think we are ready to be in the same room?" she asked.

"Janiece, it has to happen. She is the mother of my kids. We have to do this."

She sighed. "Okay," she said, and they ended the call.

She made dinner and then got the baby down when she got in. She went down to talk to her man, and he surprised her with good news. Their plans to marry in

Vegas were even better because he managed to reserve the same house they stayed in on their first trip. They continued to chat, and then the bell sounded. He went for the door, and Janiece went for the wine. Before she knew it, Kimberly was in the kitchen with her, and K.P. did not walk in behind her. "Damn," she mumbled under her breath.

"Do you mind pouring me one?" Kimberly asked, pulling out the stool from the island and then taking a seat.

"No," she replied, and went for another wineglass. She poured the golden liquid until it hit the halfway mark of the goblet, and then she placed it on the counter in front of Kimberly. Kimberly grabbed it and took a quick sip.

"This is good," she complimented it with a little nod.

"It's one of my favorites," she said, hoping she didn't sound as nervous as she was. She hadn't seen the evil one in a very long time and had no idea how this reunion would go.

"Mine too," she said with a smile and then took another sip. "Congratulations on the baby. The kids talk about her nonstop. They rave about having the cutest baby sister."

"Thanks. I had no idea that they referred to her as their little sister."

"It kinda surprised me too, but I guess she is since you and Kerry are going to be married soon."

"I guess you are right," she agreed and then took a sip. She was waiting for Kimberly to show her claws.

"Listen, the reason I wanted to be alone with you for a few moments is I have some things I need to say."

Awww shit, Janiece thought. She knew this bitch was still evil as hell. This pint-sized heifer couldn't act right for shit. "Like what?" Janiece said and shifted her weight to the right side of her body. She was preparing for the verbal brawl they'd have.

"We have a horrible past, and things got really ugly. I behaved like a lunatic, and I was so out of control that I cringe every time I think of the horrible things I did. I am so sorry for everything," she said.

Janiece thought her ears were deceiving her. This apology was not happening. No way was this monster renewed.

"What I did to your sister haunts me more than you know, and I hate that I was just that far gone. I don't know if you and I will ever be girlfriends or if you will ever grow to like me. I just wanted you to know that I'm not that person anymore. I am finally happy with myself. Back then, I was miserable, and the shit I did was crazy as fuck, and I am truly sorry."

Janiece just stood there blinking, searching for the right words to say, but she had nothing. She downed the rest of her drink and then poured another. They were quiet for a moment, but Janiece finally found her voice. "I am standing here looking you in the face wondering who you are and what you've done to Kimberly."

Kimberly laughed.

"It's true."

"I know, and I can understand. I was horrible and a mean-ass ol' mess, but therapy, my kids, my husband, and K.P. helped me to find some damn sanity. My parents and I are still a work in progress, but I'm working daily to mend that relationship with them."

Janiece nodded and then sipped.

"Lastly, I'm glad you came back to him. He has loved you so deeply and so much, and I never had that with him. He was always meant to be with you," she said, giving Janiece a smile, and Janiece swore that that was the first time she saw a smile on that woman's face.

"I know, and I guess things just were meant for us. Losing my husband and everything I had was tough, but

K.P. just rescued me, and I almost missed out due to fear and guilt, but I'm where I am supposed to be."

"I heard, and I am sorry for your loss."

"Thanks," she replied.

"I just want us to move forward. We have Kerry and the kids in common, so we must be family. I don't want there to be any weird energy when we have to be together."

"Neither do I, and I accept your apologies. I owe you one too. I was dead wrong for sleeping with Kerry when he was your husband. My behavior was low and foul, and I am sorry," she said and raised her glass.

Kimberly tapped her glass with hers, and they smiled and sipped. Janiece didn't think they'd be best friends or anything close, but for the sake of family, they had to get along.

"Hey, Kim, the kids will be down in a second," K.P. said, walking into the kitchen with the baby.

"She's awake?" Janiece asked.

"Yeah, you didn't hear her crying?"

"No, I didn't," she replied, and K.P. handed the baby to her.

"Awww, she is adorable, just like the kids bragged. May I?" Kim asked with outreached arms. Janiece paused and wanted to say hell no, but she walked around the island and handed her to her. "Wow, she is gorgeous. I remember when my kids were this little. Kayla was the sweetest baby, but that K.J. used to cry so damn much," she said.

"Yes, that boy could cry for hours," K.P. concurred, and Janiece watched how normal they seemed. Maybe all was good.

"Mom," Kayla said when she entered the kitchen. She walked over and planted a kiss on her cheek.

"Hey, baby girl," Kim returned, and then K.J. was there to greet her. They doted on the baby for a while, and then Kimberly left with the kids. Janiece whipped up

some tacos, and they ate with nonstop laughter. After she
bathed the baby and got her down, she went to join K.P.
on the sofa.

"You okay?"

"Yeah, just thinking about the Lawtons and this crazy
DNA bullshit. They think I'm that triflin' to get pregnant
by you when Isaiah got deployed. I'm just really disappointed. At one point, I had so much respect for Mr.
Lawton, and shit with Iyeshia was never solid, but they
are Jaiden's family. She already lost her daddy before
meeting him, and her kinfolk are terrible. I just want the
results to come back so they can stop looking at me like
I'm some kind of harlot. And when Iyeshia noticed my
ring, it was an entirely different issue with them."

"I said to stop worrying about them. It will be their
loss if they don't want to participate in Jaiden's life. And
Jaiden will be loved. She has us."

She knew he was right, but she wanted her daughter
to know Isaiah's family too. Isaiah would want that. K.P.
pulled her into his arms and kissed her. He smiled at her.

"Why are you smiling?"

"Because I am happy. I have you and the kids, the
company that I worked so hard to have, and it is lucrative.
I have everything I've ever wanted, and it would be so
cool if we just did it, Janiece."

"Just do what?"

"Got married. I want you to be my wife. We should just
pack a bag and do it. Kim has the kids, and we can go this
weekend."

"K.P., what about the baby?"

"I'm sure Janelle won't mind, or Ms. Phyllis. Jai, I just
want to make you my wife."

She looked at the sincerity in his eyes. "Baby, you're
serious?"

"So serious."

She hesitated for a moment and then said, "Okay."

He pulled her in and kissed her passionately, and she let him take her right there on the sofa. It felt better than the last time, and she was embracing her new life. She'd always carry Isaiah in her heart, but K.P. was there and giving her all the love that she needed, so she allowed herself to move on.

She reached out to Janelle about keeping the baby, but Janelle said she had plans she couldn't break. Janiece knew it was her extramarital affair, so she had to trust Ms. Phyllis. She stressed to K.P. that she thought that Phyllis could take care of Jaiden, but she didn't want to leave her for four days unless she was with Janelle and Greg. He then just decided that Phyllis and Jaiden would go with them.

She smiled brightly at her future. She was over the moon with joy, something she never thought she'd feel again, and nothing could erase the glow she possessed at that moment.

Chapter Twenty-three

Janelle

Before Greg arrived, she rushed to get dressed and out of the house. The kids were already sleeping, and the sitter knew to tell Greg she was going out for cocktails with her sister. She texted Devon to let him know that she was on her way. She tossed her phone into her Louie and then put on her shoes and coat. She finally did a mirror check, grabbed her handbag, and quickly exited her house. She was glad she made it away from her block before Greg got home because she didn't want to hear his complaints about never being at home anymore and how she needed to stop living her best life.

She was having the best time with Devon, and after he had introduced her to his daughter, she felt they were getting closer and she had to come clean. Living a double life wasn't easy, but she kept her lies going without many questions. She knew it was wrong, but she didn't know how to say the words, "I'm married with two kids."

"Damn, how did I get here?" she questioned as she weaved through traffic. "I have to tell him tonight," she told herself. "Yes, just explain everything, and he will understand. Yeah, he cares about me, and he will understand why I didn't tell him the truth," she convinced herself. She cranked her music and sang along with the old track "Memory Lane."

***

Greg pulled into the garage and sighed. His wife's car wasn't there again. He figured she was out with Janiece again, but he was disappointed because he felt the distance between them and wanted to try to make things right. He wanted to take her out and just talk and work on fixing things because he loved his wife and wanted them to return to the way they used to be. Their connection was lost, and he wanted them to find it again.

After he sent the babysitter home, he loosened his tie and went for a beer. He had had a long day, but that did not deter him from wanting to come home and spend that evening with his wife. He put his beer down and went up to peep in on the twins. They were sleeping, so he went back down and grabbed the remote before flopping down on the sofa in their family room.

He grabbed his phone and texted Janelle. Hey, baby, I'm home. I was hoping 2 talk and 2 spend some long overdue time with u. I don't know how, but we hve 2 get bck 2 the loving couple we were. I luv ya, he typed and added a heart-kiss emoji. A second later, he heard Janelle's ringtone sound. He felt the vibration from the alert and reached down to the area where the sound and vibration came from.

He looked at her alerts on the notification window, and right under his text, there was a text from a Devon that read, Where r u, babe? He instantly tried to open her phone, but he didn't know her PIN. He tried the twins' birthday, and it didn't work. He tried her birthday and had no luck. He tried their security alarm PIN and nothing happened, and he didn't want to get locked out, so he let the phone rest for a few minutes. He went to try again and tried their anniversary, and he was still wrong. On his last attempt after his birthday, he tried her dad's, and the phone opened. He went straight to her messages and began to scroll. A fretful look came on his face as he read the messages between a woman and her lover.

"Son of a bitch!" he yelled, and his eyes instantly watered. He would not believe that Janelle would cheat on him in a million years. The phone went off again with another text from her lover: The door is open, just come in.

Greg wanted to confirm it was what he thought it was, so he texted, What do you have planned for us?

Devon: Dinner, R&B, wine, hot bath, and you know I got this D.

Greg began to sob. He took deep breaths to calm down, but that hurt. Janelle was his wife, and he loved her, but she was allowing another man to fuck her, he thought, and he ran to the trash can and vomited. The idea of her with another man made him sick. He went over to the sink, rinsed his mouth, and then dried his face and hands with a paper towel. He had to deal with this shit. He snatched up her phone and called him.

"Hey, baby, what is taking you so long?" the male voice answered.

"I ain't yo' baby. This is Janelle's husband, Greg!" Greg thundered.

"I'm sorry?" Devon replied.

"You heard me. I am her husband."

"Is this some kind of sick joke?" Devon asked.

"No, and since she is on her way for dinner, wine, and the D, I'll catch up with you until she gets there."

"Listen, I don't know what you are talking about. Janelle is single."

"No, married with two damn kids. A set of twins!" Greg blasted.

"Come again? Janelle has kids?"

"Oh, she didn't mention them? My name is Gregory Peoples, and Janelle and I have been married for ten years, and our twins will soon be four years old. Now I don't know what lies she has told you, but she is very married and a mother to a boy and girl," Greg informed him. For a few moments, the line was silent.

"I can't fuckin' believe this shit!" Devon roared. "Listen, Gregory, my name is Devon Vanpelt, and I met Janelle about six months ago. I had no idea she was married, man. My mind is blown. I don't fuck with married women, and I promise on everything I didn't know."

"Well, I don't know how you didn't, but I guess she is good at cheating."

"I don't know, but I can assure you that I would have never gotten involved with her if I knew she was married. I'm not that guy. That is not how I do things," he said.

There was a tap on Devon's door. He rushed over to open it. Janelle was standing there gorgeous as usual, and Devon waved for her to come in. "As a matter of fact, she is here now. Do you want to talk to her?"

"Yes, please put her on," Greg said, and Devon put him on speaker.

"Who is it, Deja?" Janelle asked, taking the phone as she put her handbag on the bench near his door. "Hello," she sang.

"No, it's not Deja. It's your husband," he blasted, and the look on Janelle's face was as if she had seen a ghost.

"Oh, my God, Greg," she said in a panic.

"Yes, Greg, and the last time I checked, you were a married woman, so why are you fucking Devon? You sat here and accused me every fucking day, but you're out here riding dick, Janelle," he yelled.

Janelle fell onto the bench next to her purse. "Oh, my God, Greg. I'm sorry. I didn't want you to find out like this," she cried.

"Bring your cheating ass home right now!" he barked and ended the call.

She looked at Devon and put the phone down. "Devon, I can explain," she said, standing.

"Okay, explain. I really want to hear this shit. Fucking married with two damn kids," he yelled, holding up two fingers. "Yeah, I got to hear your explanation for this bullshit," he demanded. He was all the way in and feeling her deeply. At moments he thought he was falling in love again.

"I was hurt, and I was upset, and he was coming home later and later. The night we met, I had caught him out with a woman he claimed was a client, yet he wouldn't introduce me and basically told me to leave as if I weren't his wife. I felt like shit, and then I met you. You were great, kind, and easy to talk to, and I enjoyed us. I never intended to get this deep with you, but it just happened. Believe me, I wanted to come clean, but I was too afraid to. I'm so sorry, Devon. I started falling for you, and then we are here," she cried.

"Janelle, we've had conversations about a future together, children, and I introduced you to my daughter. I never take women around Deja unless they mean something to me. Did you not see me falling for you? How could you continue to lie when you saw us growing closer? How long did you think you could fuckin' hide a whole husband and two damn kids?" he bellowed.

"I don't know!" she yelled so loud he was sure his neighbors could hear.

"Get out!" he yelled back, pointing at the door.

"Devon, please, let's just talk. I'm so sorry for lying to you. You have to understand what I was going through with Gregory, and I didn't mean to hurt you."

"But you did, and only a narcissistic person would keep standing here trying to convince me that what you were going through excused you deceiving me. I'm asking nicely to get your ass on the other side of my door. I never want to see your ass again, Janelle."

"Devon, please don't say that."

"Goodbye, Janelle," he roared.

She reached for her handbag and walked out the door.

Devon fought the tears because he felt betrayed, but then he stopped and realized that karma had caught up to his ass, and it was time to get back the bullshit he had given.

Janelle drove home afraid to death. She was sure Greg would whip her cheating ass, and she wondered if she should just go to her sister's. She dug around in her purse, trying to find her phone, and realized she didn't have it. She figured it landed on the sofa and not in her purse when she aimlessly tossed it. That was the only way he could have known, and she wished she had made her password something random instead of a loved one's birthday.

When she pulled into the garage, her hands were trembling. She didn't have a line of defense because she was cold busted, and she didn't have any excuses to defend her adulterous behavior. When she walked into the kitchen, Gregory was in the family room on the sofa with a glass in hand and the bottle of Crown on the coffee table. She knew he probably had ten shots in the forty-five minutes she took to get home. Trembling, she slowly approached, and she was scared to even speak. After standing there with her heart pumping rapidly against her terrified chest, she said, "I'm so sorry, Greg."

He slowly lifted his head to look at her. "That's all you got? It took you damn near an hour to get here, and that is all the fuck you came up with?" he asked with tear-filled eyes.

She lowered her head in shame because she knew she hurt him, and no amount of apologies would erase her infidelity. She was sorry in all the ways one could be, and she knew that this was about to be a hard road to travel with her husband. "I didn't mean to—" she tried to say, but he cut her off quick.

"To what? Fuck another man?" his voice thundered. He picked up her cell phone and began to scroll through her text messages. "'I miss you, boo, can't wait to see you either. I had a good time last night, and daddy, you got me wet just thinking about it,'" he recited, and she was so embarrassed that her husband saw all the intimate bullshit she shared with another man that she just covered her face and sobbed into her hands. Hearing all the unfaithful conversations she had shared with Devon made her sick to her stomach.

Before she knew it, her phone flew across the room and hit the wall. He launched off the sofa and was in her face within seconds. He scared the fuck out of her. She thought this would be the first time he put his hands on her. He stood in her face breathing deeply, and she knew he was infuriated. After a moment, he backed up a couple of spaces. "Janelle, this is the ultimate betrayal, baby, and I can't even look at your ass right now. In all the stress of this bullshit ass of marriage and the aggravations and pain you have caused me, I've never once fucked another woman. Did shit cross my mind? Yes, but I'd never do that to you, woman, because I fuckin' love you so much."

"Greg, you stopped touching me, and you—" she tried to say, and he cut her off.

"No, don't you fucking dare put your infidelity on me," he yelled. "Don't you even attempt to justify letting another man fuck you because of this illusion you've had in your head of what you assumed I was doing," he barked. "The bottom line is I had my fuckin' issues with this marriage, and shit swam around in my head about if our marriage would make it, and even though I've had opportunities to fuck, I've never," he spat at her.

"How do I know that?" she yelled.

"Because I say so, Janelle, and as mad as I am right now at your cheating ass, I can't even lie to even the fuckin' score. I am so angry with you, and if you weren't the mother of my children, I'd shake the shit out of you!"

She trembled at his words. "Gregory, I didn't know, and I didn't trust you anymore," she cried. "Things had changed, and we were not us, and you acted as if you were no longer interested in me or this marriage. I expressed what I felt, but you ignored it."

"Okay, with that. You didn't trust me. You thought I was fucking other women, yet you had no proof at all, but just say I really was. Does that make what you did with Devon right?" he asked, getting in her face again. "No, it doesn't, and I am done with you. I am done with this marriage. You are free to ride Devon's dick all night long from now on," he said and took off his ring. He dropped it on the floor and walked away.

He headed for the steps, and Janelle ran behind him, begging him not to leave, but that was no use because he quickly packed two suitcases and didn't acknowledge her cries and apologies. He was at the door, and she was by the island, her face drenched with tears. She was still whispering, "Please don't go," but she knew nothing she could say would make him stay.

"Know this," he said before making his exit. "I was aware our marriage was on the road to disaster, but I thought you loved me enough to try to fix our issues. Never in a zillion years did I think our marriage would encounter infidelity."

"Baby, please don't go. I fucked up, and I love you. Please don't leave like this, Greg. I want to fix it now. Just please stay. We can figure our shit out. I need us back."

"You ruined that chance for us," he said and then walked out.

She fell to the floor and sobbed so hard. Janiece told her months ago to shut that shit down, but she was feeling herself and doing what she thought was the same thing Greg was doing, but she was so wrong, and her husband was heartbroken and never coming back. She had fucked Devon over with her stupid lies. She now saw how it felt to walk in someone else's shoes. She judged Janiece and K.P. for years, but she was no better.

She went for the wine and drank and cried until she passed out. The next morning the twins woke her. She realized she was on the sofa and the night before was not a dream.

Chapter Twenty-four

Janiece

Janelle was a wreck, and Janiece was right there by her side. She avoided saying, "I told you so," and she just went by every other day to check on Janelle. Greg had been gone for two months, and it looked like he wasn't coming back.

"It hurts so bad," Janelle cried, sitting at the kitchen table and looking a mess. Her curls were dry, and her face was pale. She looked as though she had lost fifteen or more pounds. "He only comes for the kids. He won't even talk to me." She continued to sob.

Her sister was in bad shape, and she hated seeing her like that. "Janelle, you have to give it time. Greg is hurt and upset right now. He needs time, sis, to get past the pain. Eventually, y'all will talk about it. He hasn't mentioned divorce, so there is a chance that you two will work it out," Janiece assured her, trying to be positive.

"No, we won't, sissy. You didn't see the way he looked at me when he left. It was like I wasn't shit to him. Gregory has never looked at me with that much disdain, and he hates me now, Janiece. I should have listened to you when you told me to get out of my head. I just used Devon to feel like I wasn't being played. All of my decisions were stupid as fuck, and I love my husband, Janiece, and I want him back so bad. I should have never done that shit to him, and every time I try to talk about us, he hangs up, walks out, or replies with something totally unrelated to the words I have said. I'm so fucking sorry." She cried harder.

Janiece stood and went around to embrace her older sister. "Shhh, come on now, sissy, it's going to be okay. You have to be positive and just give Greg some time. He is crazy about you and madly in love with you, and he is hurt. I mean, you have to realize that what you did takes a minute to return from. Once he gets past the pain, y'all will figure it out. Just prepare yourself for whatever he decides because if you had caught him doing exactly what you did, you'd be treating him the same exact way. Please stop thinking about and focusing on what you feel. Put yourself in his shoes, and be patient with him."

"I hate it when you are right," she joked and laughed.

"I have my moments," Janiece playfully returned.

"I will get it together and allow him to process and decide. I don't deserve him. All I had was empty accusations, and I went with that and got close to another man. Devon didn't deserve my bullshit either," she said, finally taking some ownership of her bullshit.

"No, he didn't, and I warned you."

"You did, and if Greg wants a divorce, I will not fight it. I'm getting everything I deserve," she said, and Janiece nodded. "Damn, Jai, no, that's not true?"

"Nope, because you are. I remember when I showed my ass with K.P. at that New Year's Eve party. When Isaiah told me to kick rocks. I brought that shit on myself. I had to take that shit at face value."

"But at least y'all got back together and got married."

"We did, but I couldn't predict my future, and neither can you. You and Greg are so up in the air."

"You're right." She nodded.

"I want you to come out of this funk and get back to living. All this depression shit won't make him decide one way or the other. I got to get home to my hubby."

"How is that going, Mrs. Paxton?"

"Perfect. Every day has been bliss." She smiled.

"I am happy for you, sis."

"Thank you, and I love you. You know you and the twins are welcome whenever you want to get out. I'm a stay-at-home mom, so anytime you want to, drop by."

"Thanks. Now that it's getting warmer, we can sit by that gorgeous pool and drink tropical drinks."

"Absolutely," she agreed, grabbing her designer bag, shades, and keys. "Bye, kiddos," she yelled to her niece and nephew.

"Bye, Auntie Jai," they both said in unison.

She made her exit and climbed into her new Mercedes. K.P. surprised her with it as a wedding gift. She felt terrible because she had not thought to get him anything since their wedding was so last-minute. She later spent way too much on an engraved watch for him, but he deserved it.

She was happy to see her husband cooking dinner when she walked in. The aroma filled the house, and her nose was pleased.

"Hey, babe," she said and put her purse on the counter.

"Hey, you, welcome home," he said, and she went over to steal a kiss.

"What are you making?"

"My famous spaghetti," he said proudly.

"Well, it smells amazing, baby, and I am hungry," she said and took a seat at the kitchen island. Her eyes landed on a UPS envelope with her name on it. "What's this?" she asked, grabbing it.

"Not sure. It came for you earlier."

She proceeded to open it. She pulled out the letter and fell back onto her stool.

"What is it, baby? What's wrong?" K.P. questioned.

"No, God, this can't be happening. What in the fuck is wrong with these people?" she huffed.

"Jai, tell me what it says."

"Isaiah's family demands full custody of my baby," she answered.

"No fucking way," K.P. said and turned off the burner. "Let me see that. On what grounds?" he asked, taking the letter from her hands. His eyes scanned the document, and it was true. "These bitches keep coming for us, Janiece, and this shit right here is ludicrous. This bullshit about you not being financially stable enough to take care of Jaiden is some bullshit. Everything I have is yours, so this right here ain't gon' work."

"Can they take my baby, K.P.?" she asked, terrified. The Lawtons were far from broke.

"No, and they will have a hell of a fight if they try us with this bullshit. You are not some broke widow without resources, so don't worry your pretty little head about this, babe," K.P. said and kissed the side of her head. She trusted him and believed he would take care of it like he always did. She allowed him to give her a tight hug and a wet kiss before he returned to cooking. She went up to see her baby.

After dinner, and after the kids were down, they sat by the pool, and K.P. held her as tight as he could and assured her that things would be fine. He would forward the documents to Marcus the next morning to confirm they were legit, and whatever it took to shut the Lawtons down, he assured Janiece he'd do.

A few weeks later, the judge denied the Lawtons' full custody request and gave them visitation. As soon as they walked out of the courtroom, Iyeshia had to give Janiece her parting words.

"You're a fucking piece of work, Janiece," she yelled, and Janiece stopped. She was exhausted with her. "You married that muthafucka in June and didn't say a word to us. You ain't shit. I know Jaiden is a Lawton, but you still ain't shit."

"I don't owe you or your family a report or explanation of what I do or who I do it with. Y'all kicked me out of my home, not giving a damn where my daughter and I would live, and didn't give me a single bit of my husband's insurance money. So I don't owe you or your father shit," Janiece yelled.

"You are a funky-ass, whore-ass bitch. Why my brother loved you, I'll never understand. You left with that nigga the day of my brother's funeral, and not six months later you married him, so fuck you, Janiece. If you were not my niece's mother, I'd beat the shit outta you. You didn't love my brother and should have stayed with that nigga you married instead of pretending that Isaiah meant anything to you. He is the one you've always wanted," she barked.

"Iyeshia, that's not true, and you don't know what Isaiah and I had," she tried to say.

"Y'all had nothing. You are so evil, and I hate my brother's feelings for your ass," she said and stormed off. "Fuck you, Janiece," she yelled as she walked toward the exit.

Janiece stood defeated again. There was no winning with the Lawtons.

"Come on, baby, let's go home," K.P. said, pulling her to him. She just let him take care of her from that moment on.

Chapter Twenty-five

Iyeshia

Iyeshia was at her parents' house helping her mom in the kitchen when the phone rang. She went over to the old phone her parents still had on the kitchen wall.

"Hello," she answered.

"Janiece Lawton, please," the man requested.

"She's not here. Can I help you with something?"

"This is Staff Sergeant Morris. Is Isaac or Doreen Lawton available?" he inquired.

"Yes, my mom is." Iyeshia wanted to know what it was about, so she told her mom to get the cordless phone.

"Hello, this is Doreen Lawton," she said.

"Hello Mrs. Lawton, this call is about your son, Captain Isaiah Lawton."

"Yes, okay. My son died a little while ago. What is this about?"

"Well, ma'am, that is what we thought, but he is alive, and we need to notify his wife and family that he will be home soon."

"Is this some kind of sick joke? It's not funny, sir," Doreen said. "The uniformed men came to my daughter-in-law's home, and we had a funeral. This has to be a mix-up," she expressed, and Iyeshia knew she was upset, but she wanted the man to give them more information.

"I can understand your doubt, but your son was a POW and is coming home within the next couple of days."

Doreen fell back against the wall, and Iyeshia hung up the phone and rushed to aid her mother. She took the cordless and explained to the man who she was and that the news had her mother overwhelmed. He understood and informed her of a few more details and told her they'd be able to talk to him soon. She hung up.

Her mom was now on the floor weeping. "My baby boy is alive. He is alive," she said.

When they got up and processed the news, they called Isaac, and he hurried home. By the time Isaiah was on the line, everyone was overjoyed to hear his voice, and he asked a million times about Janiece. Doreen jumped in, feeding him a bunch of lies that she was on vacation somewhere with the baby, and Iyeshia shook her head. When the call ended, Iyeshia addressed the lies. He told his mom not to tell her he was coming home because he wanted to surprise her. Doreen agreed with him because she didn't want him to get the news of her and K.P. being back together while he was still overseas.

"Momma, why did you lie to him and not tell him?" she said.

"His heart is going to be broken, and he needs to be here for that type of heartache, Iyeshia. We have no idea what your brother has been through, so no, he will learn the truth when he is home and I can wrap my arms around my boy and be here for him." Doreen sighed.

"I get it, ma, but I hate it."

"So do I, and again I'll say that Janiece is not wrong for moving on."

"Ma, why do you constantly defend that . . ." She wanted to say "bitch," but she didn't.

"Janiece explained to me what your issue is with her. People grieve differently, and you and your stubborn father went into accusatory mode. She left that man and married Isaiah, but she gets no credit for that. They tried for months to conceive, and your niece is here, and DNA proved it, yet you and your father want to keep treating my grandchild like a bastard. She thought your brother was dead. She didn't cheat. So I am tired of your and Isaac's hatred for this woman. Your brother chose her. And they had a good marriage."

"Whatever, ma. You don't know her, and I do. When Isaiah gets home, he will see the same thing," she said and left the kitchen.

Chapter Twenty-six

Isaiah

When the plane landed, he was so happy to finally be back on American soil. He was anxious to go home and was excited to see his daughter. He was a dad, and the will to live for his wife and daughter gave him the strength to make it through all he had gone through, and for it to finally be over confirmed his belief in the Most High. He wasn't all in one piece the way he left, but he was healthy and alive.

He deboarded, and there was a car waiting for him. The government was so secretive that his family had no idea what day or time he'd arrive. He was ready to surprise his girls, so he rode quietly in the back of the car. Once he arrived home, things were strange. The grass was overgrown, and there were numerous newspapers out front. He asked the driver to wait, and he grabbed his cane and got out. He went to the door, and it was locked, so he went to the windows to find an empty home. "What in the fuck is going on?" he asked and then headed back to the car. He asked the driver to take him to his mom and rode with a million thoughts in his head.

At his parents', he got out with his cane, and the driver got out and retrieved his duffle bag from the trunk. He slowly walked up the driveway, and when he got to the door, he was happy to see that it was open. He walked in, and everything was the same, the way he remembered. He made his way to the kitchen, following his nose.

When Doreen saw him, she dropped the glass bowl she had in her hands. She ran over to him. "My son, my son, my baby boy, my son," she said and then began to sob. She held him for countless minutes, and he held her. Finally, she let go, caressed his face, and pulled him in tightly for a hug. When she finally let him go, he wanted to know where his wife and child were and why they were not in their home, so he said, "I am so happy to be back, and I am anxious to meet my kid. Do you know where they are or what happened?"

"Son, have a seat," she suggested, and he immediately assumed that something terrible had happened to them.

"No, I can't sit. Where is my family?"

"With K.P.," Iyeshia blurted, walking into the kitchen at the end of his question. He went to hug his sister because he was happy to see her. They exchanged "I missed yous," and she thanked God he was home.

When he pulled away, he asked her, "Did you say my wife was with K.P.?" He leaned in as if he had not heard her right.

"Yes, and they are engaged," Iyeshia spat.

"Engaged? My wife is engaged? My wife and kid are in Las Vegas?"

"Wait, son, but before you get all upset, let me explain, and no, they are not in Vegas."

"How could she?" he asked, moving over to take a seat. The news was like a shot to his heart. Before his mother could tell him what was going on, Iyeshia gladly gave him her version of the story, making Janiece look like a cheating whore.

"No, no, son, it didn't go exactly that way. Now, Iyeshia, why are you telling your brother this exaggerated story?"

"It's the truth, ma, and you just keep defending that tramp," she spat.

"I need to talk to her. I need to see her."

"I know exactly where they are. I've taken Mom over there to see the baby," she said.

"Take me to them," he said, standing.

"Isaiah, I don't think that it is a good idea to just show up. She doesn't even know that you're alive. Remember, you asked me not to tell her because you wanted to surprise her," his mother reminded him.

"That was before I knew she ran back to K.P."

Doreen followed him, trying to stop him. "Wait, son, there is more," she said, and he paused.

"What do you mean, more? What more can there be?" Doreen's eyes watered, and he knew it would be something to hurt him even more. "Mom, what is the more?"

"They are married, son."

"Married!" Isaiah and Iyeshia blurted.

"Yes, they are married."

Isaiah fell back against the wall, just putting his head down and rubbing the top of his head. He was just trying to process what she said to him. His eyes burned with tears.

"Son," Doreen said and reached for him, but he held up his hand.

It took him a moment, but he then stood, wiped his face with a couple of swipes, and blew out a deep breath. He didn't know what to think. He just knew he had to get to her and bring her home. Once she knew he was alive, things would go back to the way they were, he told himself. He said, "Let's go," and headed toward the door.

"Son, I don't—" she tried to say, but he cut her off.

"Ma, I'm going to get my family," he said, not looking back at her.

They rode to K.P. and Janiece's house with Iyeshia giving him the entire story of K.P. showing up at the gravesite and how Janiece wasted no time running back to him. Isaiah just had to see her and talk to her. He knew it had to be something different from what his sister had told him. She never liked Janiece to start with. He just wanted to get to her.

Once they parked, he asked for her phone. She unlocked it and gave it to him. He dialed her number, and it was not in service. "Do you know her new number?"

"It's programmed in there," she said and took her phone. She scrolled and hit call, and when she gave it to Isaiah, the screen read Bitch. He shook his head and then waited for her to answer. When she didn't, he called again. And still, she didn't answer. He went to her text messages and texted, Urgent pls call me ASAP. Five minutes later, when she didn't call, he called again.

"What do you want, Iyeshia?"

"Jai," he said.

"Hello," she said.

"Hey, Jai, baby, it's me," he said, blinking back tears. It felt good to hear her voice.

"You know what? Tell Iyeshia this shit isn't funny," she said and hung up. He dialed her again. When she answered, he put her on speaker.

"What kind of sick joke is this?" she spat.

"Janiece, I'm not joking. It is Isaiah, and we are outside," Iyeshia said.

"What? What?" she said and ended the call.

"What now?" Iyeshia asked, and he just stared at the phone.

Before he could speak, the front door opened, and he laid eyes on his wife.

Chapter Twenty-seven

Janiece

She dropped her phone and hurried to the front door. When she opened it, a car was sitting in their drive, so she stepped out and started walking toward it. Her hands trembled at the idea of that being him. It sounded for sure like him, but it couldn't be.

The car door opened, and a man in uniform stepped out. It was her husband. Before she could stop herself, she ran into his arms and sobbed while he held her tight. "Oh, my God. Oh, my God, this can't be real," she cried.

"It's real, baby, and I am real," he said, and she let him kiss her ten times before he let her go. She was so overtaken by emotions that she forgot about her entire current situation.

"How, I mean, what? What?" she cried. "My heart and mind are racing right now."

"I feel the same, and I missed you so much. Where is my little girl? I can't wait for another second to see her."

"Of course. I guess you can come in, and I am sure they have updated you on everything."

"Unfortunately, yes, but none of that matters right now. I just want to lay eyes on my daughter," he stressed.

"Come on," she said, and they headed toward the door. "K.P. is home," she warned. He continued to follow her inside. "Have a seat, and I'll be right back."

She headed straight to K.P.'s office first because he had no clue what was happening. "Kerry, stop whatever you are doing and listen to me."

He looked up and recognized trouble in her expression. He asked, "Babe, what is it?"

"Isaiah. Isaiah is . . . Isaiah is . . ." she tried to say, but the tears started again. She began pacing, and her hands were shaking.

He stood and came to pull her into a hug. "Baby, it's okay. I know you have your moments, and it's okay."

"No, Kerry, he is alive." She finally pushed those words out.

"Wait, baby, what are you talking about?" he asked, pulling away.

"He is here, right now, in our living room. Isaiah is not dead," she expressed.

"Are you serious right now, Janiece?"

"Yes. He just called me from our driveway, and I have no clue what is going on, but he is here."

"Well, I'll be damned," he said.

"I have to go up and get Jaiden. He wants to see her."

"Of course, of course," he said, and they both exited his office. He decided to wait for Janiece at the bottom of the stairs.

She came down with the baby, and they went into the living room. Isaiah grabbed a cane Janiece didn't even realize he had and hoisted himself up from the sofa. She walked over to him and handed him a sleeping Jaiden. He let his cane go and took her into his arms. He wiped tears away as he admired her. "She is so beautiful, and I can't believe that I am finally holding my baby girl," he said, pulling her close to his face. "Can I sit?"

"Yes, of course," K.P. said, and Isaiah looked at him. "Good to have you home, man," K.P. said.

"Good to be home," he returned and then took a seat. He just caressed the baby's face and just held her close to his face.

Janiece took a seat, and K.P. exited the room. Janiece was happy he gave them some space. "Listen, I know you want to spend time with her, so you can take her back with you for a few days. I'm okay with that."

"What about you? When are you coming home?"

"Isaiah, I am married to K.P. now, and it's not that simple."

"It is that simple, Janiece. I'm your husband, and I am not going to just let you go like that," he said, and the baby stirred. He lowered his voice and said, "You know I love you, Janiece, and I want my family home with me."

"Listen, I'll find time to come and talk to you. I can't just up and leave."

"Why not, huh? I'm your husband, and as effed up as things are," he said, lowering his tone again, "I want my wife and daughter, and I don't want to leave here tonight without the both of you. Do you know how much I love you and how long I have waited to see you again? That is the only thing that kept me alive, Jai, and I'm not going to sit here and say, 'Okay, stay with K.P.' That is not happening," he said.

Tears welled in her eyes again. She felt for him, and at that moment, she knew she still loved him, but she had fallen in love again with K.P.

"Please, Isaiah, don't do this tonight. I can't make any decisions tonight. I have a hard time processing that you are even here. I can't drop everything and just do that to K.P.," she stressed.

"So damn me and our marriage and what we have?"

"No, Isaiah, you know damn well that is not how I feel about you, so don't say shit like that to me. This is a lot to figure out, and we can't do that in one night."

"You're right," he said and swiped at his tears. "At least I can bond with my daughter, so can you just pack her things so I can go?" he asked, looking at the baby and not at Janiece.

"Sure. Can you come with me to her nursery?"

"Yeah," he said low and grabbed his cane.

"I can take her," Janiece offered.

"Your man is a soldier. I can manage," he said and was up in a matter of seconds. He climbed the steps behind Janiece with his cane in his right hand and his baby girl in his left. When they walked inside Jaiden's room, he complimented how beautiful it was.

"Thanks," Janiece said and began to pack her baby's things.

"This is what I imagined we'd do at our house for her," he added.

"Yeah, the house your family threw us out of," she mumbled. It was too much to talk about that night, so she did not want to share how horribly they'd treated her.

"What was that?" he asked.

"Nothing," she said and continued to get Jaiden's bag ready. "This is her daddy book. I know you are home, and she is going to be confused when she wakes and sees you, but we go through this book every night before she goes to sleep," she said, opening the book. She turned the pages so he could see.

"You tell her who I am?"

"Yes. I found this online and got one made for her. She knows that you are her daddy," she said. "I will give you two a little time to bond, and then I will come by so we can talk."

"Janiece, it is killing me that you are not going home. Why you got back with him is obvious. You've only loved him and me, so I get it, but you chose me, remember? You married me, so it is breaking my heart that I'm leaving with half of my family. I just want to kiss you so bad," he said, moving closer to her. He leaned in, and she didn't stop him. She allowed the kiss, and she kissed him back. She missed him too, so much, but she couldn't just walk out. She pulled back.

"Isaiah, you should go."

"Do you love me, Jai?"

"Isaiah, you know I do. I loved you when I was your wife, but now things are different, and I just can't walk out on K.P.," she said, and he backed away.

"Okay, and I understand more than you think I do. I've been gone for months, and you thought I was dead, but I am not going to stop pursuing you. I love you, and this is just day one. And there is a lot to be discussed, talked about, and worked out. I'll win you back because Jaiden and I are your family," he said and then leaned in to kiss her lips one more time.

He turned to walk out, and she followed him with the baby's bag. When they got back down, K.P. was surprisingly sitting in the living room talking to Iyeshia.

"I had to use the bathroom," she said when Janiece and Isaiah eyed her.

"And get a glass of wine?" Janiece asked.

"Well, K.P. offered," she said and polished off the glass.

"K.P., I need to grab Jaiden's car seat for Isaiah," Janiece said, and K.P. got up and went to get it. He walked out with Iyeshia and put it in the car.

Janiece was amazed at how Jaiden still slept during the entire ordeal. She grabbed some more things she thought he would need from the kitchen and walked them out. Iyeshia took the baby, and Isaiah stood staring at her.

"You are still so beautiful to me. And I miss touching you," he said and reached out to caress her cheek.

She laid her hand on his. "I am overjoyed that you made it back to us. Jaiden has her father, and that gives my heart so much joy, Isaiah, but I don't want to have to decide, and I don't want to break your heart."

"I made it through war, Janiece. I have survived the most horrific thing that a man could possibly go through, and I didn't fight to stay alive to come home and lose the woman I love. I will give you space to process all of this because, trust me, I need that too, but I love you, and I can't just let you go. We had plans, Janiece, and my future is with you." With that, he stole one last kiss and turned to walk away.

She stood there until their headlights turned out of their drive, and then she went inside. She went out on the patio and just stared at the swaying water in the pool. It was May, and they had warm days, but that night was chilly, but she didn't feel it. How on earth could her dead husband not be dead?

"Here you go, baby," K.P. said, handing her a glass of red, and then he draped a blanket over her shoulders.

"Thank you, bae," she said and sipped.

"Eventful evening," he said.

"You think?" she said with a light chuckle.

"Yes, and I need to know what is going on in that pretty little head of yours."

"Nothing and everything. I don't have a single clue what I should be thinking right now because every thought is mind-blowing, and I don't want to think about it right now."

"Are you going to leave me?"

She turned to him. "What, K.P.? Baby, no, leaving you is the last thing on my mind."

"He is going to want your marriage back," he returned.

"I know, Kerry, and right now, to be honest, I don't want to tackle the thoughts of that. I can't imagine hurting him all over again, so for tonight, I can't think beyond this moment I have right here with you."

"Okay, and don't worry. Things will be okay," he said, kissing her on top of her head. "Are you coming in? It's chilly, Jai."

"No, I'm gonna sit out here for a little longer. You can head inside if you want."

He sat behind her on the lounge chair and pulled her in close. "I'm going to stay out here with you and hold you," he said, and she relaxed in his arms.

Chapter Twenty-eight

Isaiah

The next couple of days were spent clearing up his mistaken death and bonding with his baby girl. Isaiah thought about Janiece morning, noon, and night, and he missed her beyond words. They talked, but it was mostly about the baby, and as soon as he'd mention anything about them, she'd find a way to end the call. He was exhausted thinking about how he'd get her back and tired of his sister bashing her every time he'd mention her name. His father was a quiet man, but he made sure to put a hand on his shoulder and tell him that he was better off without her.

He hadn't liked the fact that she went back to K.P. at all, but he knew in his heart that she had done nothing wrong. She thought he was dead, and K.P. was familiar, and he knew she loved him at one time. He shook off the thoughts of his woman being back with K.P. and pulled into the driveway of their home. He missed it and didn't want to be at his parents' house for much longer. It was great having his mom since Jaiden was familiar with her, but now Jaiden was used to him, and that daddy book made it easier. She looked at him strangely the first time, but she sang the "Da-da" song to him and smiled. That he was grateful for.

He did a walkthrough of the house and knew he needed a housekeeper to get it back to move-in ready. Janiece had come by with K.P. to give him the key to the unit she had all their things stored in. Watching her walk away and drive off with K.P. was hard, but that was what it was for now. He passed the room that was supposed to be for his daughter and saw that the walls were half done. He wondered why and when she actually moved out of their home. He went to open the closet and was pleased to see the paint and supplies were there, so he knew that it would be a priority to finish painting his daughter's room. The power and water were still on, and he was grateful for that.

He figured since Janiece had just recently gotten married, she hadn't had time to put the house up for sale. Or did she have plans to rent it out? He had so many questions. He made a mental note of the color scheme and went by the storage facility to access what Janiece had left. He noted that there were no baby furnishings, so he decided to get his baby a bed and other things for her room. He wanted her room to be as beautiful as the one she had at K.P.'s place. The saleslady was nice and helpful, and he decided to go with a toddler bed with a railing instead of a crib since she was already a year old. She wasn't an infant anymore, and he thought she was ready for it.

He went to a few other stores and got some more up-to-date electronics and then headed back to his place to paint. The furniture would be delivered the next day, so he wanted her walls to be dry. After he painted, he locked up and called it a day. He would meet the cleaning service back at the house the next morning, and after the delivery, he and a few of his friends would load a truck and move him back in. He had gotten a nice lump sum of money from the military, and he was only focused on his family for now.

Iraq stole a chunk of his life, and being a POW was not only physically tormenting but also mentally, so he had to see someone a couple days a week to help him cope with it all. With all he had gone through, he still had faith that his life would get back to normal, and all would be just fine. He returned to his mom's and was happy to see his daughter. She loved him, and he knew it because she was always happy to see him. He was so anxious to get their home together so he could take her to the home she'd grow up in.

The next morning, he was up bright and early and back at his place to meet the cleaning service. He requested a crew of four because he didn't want them there all damn day. Since the house was empty, he met up with a few of his friends, and they loaded the truck. When they made it back, the crew was finishing up, and Isaiah could see the difference. He was pleased, and when the truck was empty, one of his boys did him a huge favor and returned the truck. He had to be here for the furniture delivery, and by three that afternoon, Jaiden's room looked like a room fit for a little princess. He was proud and pleased and knew he'd go home that evening with his baby girl. The boxes were all labeled, so it didn't take long to find dishes, pots, and pans. He tackled the kitchen enough so he could at least cook meals as he slowly got the place back to normal. He headed to the grocery store, grabbed some things, and decided to unload before he picked up Jaiden. It was close to nine by the time he made it back to his parents, and although the house smelled of food, nothing was on the stove.

"Your plate is in the microwave, son," his mom said.

"Where is my daughter?" he asked.

"She is upstairs with her papa, and you need to hurry because she has been rubbing her little eyes."

He rushed upstairs and took her from his dad and gave her kisses.

"She is ready for bed, son."

"I know, but I'm taking her home tonight."

"I don't think y'all should go tonight. Just wait 'til the morning," he suggested.

Jaiden's eyes fluttered, and he thought that would be best, but he wanted her to be home to sleep in her own bed. "Nah. I'ma grab my plate, and we gon' head out," he said and left the room. He went back down and put a sleeping Jaiden in the playpen that was in his parents' living room. He went for his plate and set it on the counter. He had a few bags to get from his old room, but his mom called out to him before he went up.

"How did your last meeting go with Janiece?"

He hunched his shoulders. "As good as it could have, I guess. She always shows up with K.P., so we never really have a chance to have a real conversation."

"I'm sorry to hear that. I know this may not be what you want to hear, but there is a chance that she may not come back."

"Ma, I'm not going to even go there or let my mind entertain that thought. I know my wife, and all we need is some real time together, and I know we can rekindle our love. It will be fine," he said, looking over at his baby. "I got to have hope for us. If I stop hoping, that means I gave up, and I can't do that."

"Okay, son. I just don't want to see you hurt, that's all."

"I know," he said, and at that moment, Iyeshia walked in with two of his cousins whom he hadn't seen since he got back.

He stayed a little longer, and then he went home. He put his daughter in her bed, and after, he showered. He grabbed a couple of pillows and a blanket and lay on the floor near Jaiden's bed. He had found his old phone in a box labeled "Isaiah's stuff" that he had left behind before he deployed, and it was now fully charged. He powered it on, and the password was their wedding day, so he got in quickly. He scrolled through all of their old pictures, and his eyes glossed.

He missed everything about her: her scent, her silly habits, and how she just made him feel special. He missed making love to her, and the house felt different now that she was gone. "Please, God, let me be with my wife again. Let her love me again if that is your will. You brought me out of hell, and to go the rest of my days without my wife would be no different. If it is your will, bring her home," he prayed and then thought of his mother's words. "And if that is not your will, give me the strength to move on and send me the one who is truly meant for me. Amen," he said. He looked through her pictures for a little while longer, and then he finally fell asleep.

Chapter Twenty-nine

Janelle

"Gab, grab your brother's hand, I said," she instructed. "If I have to tell you one more time, you will get a spanking," she fussed. Her daughter did what she was told, and then she turned back to the saleslady. "Do you have this in red?" she asked, examining the phone case she was considering from a kiosk in the mall.

"Let me take a look," the woman replied and went looking in the cabinets.

An unfamiliar voice spoke from behind her, and she turned.

"Hello," Janelle replied.

"Hi, Ms. Janelle, I'm Deja, remember? Devon's daughter," she said, reminding her.

"Of course. Hey, Deja, how are you?"

"I'm fine, and this is my mom, Leila. Mom, this is dad's friend, Ms. Janelle."

"Hello," Leila spoke. No longer than a second later, Devon walked up.

"Hi," she said nervously.

"Hello, Janelle," he returned.

"How have you been?" she asked.

"Well, and you?"

"I've been good."

"These are your twins?" he asked.

"Yes, this is Gabrielle and Gregory," she said.

"Nice," he returned, and then Leila and Deja stepped away.

"Listen, Devon, I'm really sorry for what went down with us and for not being honest."

"It's all good, no worries, and I've accepted your apology, so all is good."

"He left me," she offered up.

"Ma'am, we have red," the saleslady said, interrupting.

Janelle couldn't care less about that damn case. Her attention was on Devon.

"I'm sorry to hear that, Janelle. It was great seeing you. Take care of yourself," he said and hurried over to his daughter and Leila.

She wondered if they had gotten back together. She turned to the clerk, said, "Never mind," and hurried out of the mall. She made it home, fed her kids, and after bath time, she allowed them movie time before she put them to bed. She was feeling so sad and lonely, so she called Janiece.

"Greg won't budge, Janiece, and I am so tired of begging and crying. Maybe it's time to let it go and accept it is over."

"Nellie, you can't give up hope," she encouraged her.

"It's been seven months, and I can't apologize enough or do anything to convince him to come home."

"Sis, if you want to let go, then do that. I just want you to get back to happy."

"Yeah, maybe. I ran into Devon today."

"As in affair Devon?"

"Yes, and don't say that word. I feel horrible and sick about the affair."

"I'm sorry, baby, go on."

"He spoke, I told him Gregory left, and he pretty much said to have a nice life and walked off. But he looked so damn delicious, and I ran up out of that mall, because how do I want my husband back, but then I see him and soak my damn panties?"

"I don't know because I have enough going on with my situation with my two husbands."

"The same two men fighting over you again, and I have no one," she said sadly.

"Well, I wish I didn't. I love Isaiah, and I missed him so much for so long, and now I have fallen back in love with K.P. Either way it goes, it's like we are back to six years ago when I was caught up with the both of them. I'm smack dab in the middle of K.P. and Isaiah again. I am going to Isaiah's to get the baby, and I'm terrified to be alone with him."

"Janiece, just tell him that you are going to stay with K.P."

"I've told him, but I don't want to be alone with him. When he comes close to me, it just does something to me, and that energy is still alive, and I just can't be around him long. I miss him in so many ways, but I'm so happy. It's so hard to explain."

"Oh, so you are scared that you're going to want to go back to him?"

"Yes, and it is not the pressure I need. I love K.P. so much, and I would not have fallen back this deep if I didn't think Isaiah was dead, and it kills me to hurt him, Janelle. It is so hard every day because I know he loves me, and I don't want to hurt him, but I can't have them both, either."

At that moment, Janelle's cell rang, and she looked to see that it was Devon. She put Janiece on hold and took the call. "Hello."

"Hey, Janelle, how are you?"

"I'm good."

"I just wanted to call and say that I am sorry that your marriage didn't work out. I know and understand why you lied. It was fucked up, but I do forgive you."

"Thanks, Devon. I know I did a shitty thing, but I can't go back in time or change it."

"I know, and you hurt a brother badly," he joked.

"I know," she agreed.

"I just wanted to ask if you wanted to have dinner."

Shocked, she repeated, "Dinner?"

"Yes, dinner tomorrow night if you are free."

"I am, and I'd like that," she said.

"Well, can I pick you up say around seven thirty?"

"That is perfect. I will text you my address."

"Great." They ended the call, and she went back to Janiece.

"So now I have a date," she squealed.

"Are you sure you're ready for that?"

"No, but he is showing up. The man I want won't talk to me, so I guess it's time to face reality."

"Yep, I'm afraid so."

They talked for a little while longer, and then she got off. She secured a sitter and then went to look for something to wear for tomorrow. She wasn't sure where she and Devon would go, but she was sure she was done begging.

Chapter Thirty

Janiece

Janiece pulled into the driveway of the house that she used to call home. She sat in her car for a few minutes and took deep, cleansing breaths before she got out. She approached the door and rang the bell and then nervously waited for him to open the door. When Isaiah opened the door, he was looking finer than the last time she had seen him. He had a fresh haircut and fresh shave. Janiece didn't know if she should leave and come back with K.P. because she still cared for him a great deal.

She walked inside, and so many memories flooded her mind. Isaiah had made their home look exactly like she had made it look before he deployed. She had to blink back her tears. The furniture placements and wall hangings were exactly the way she remembered them. "Wow, Isaiah, everything looks so beautiful. Like our home looked before," she admitted.

"I remembered everything like we set it all up together." He smiled. "You look gorgeous, and I am so happy to see you," he said and moved in close to her again.

She took a step back away from him because she was now with K.P. and had to set boundaries with Isaiah. He had to accept that she was not coming back.

"I know, Isaiah. Where is Jaiden?" she asked.

"She is already sleeping. I tried to keep her up, but we went to the park today, and she played hard. After I fed her and gave her a bath, she fell asleep in my arms while we were watching *SpongeBob,* so she is in her room."

"Can I go up and see her? I mean, I know you had a lot of time away, but I miss my baby too."

"Yes, and I bet," he said, and she followed him up the stairs. The house looked the same, but Jaiden's room had transformed.

"Oh, my God, Isaiah, you finished her room. It is so beautiful," Janiece said, touching things. "This is so beautiful, and I love it. This room is fit for our princess."

"It is, and it was my pleasure. I wanted her to feel at home here because this is her home, Janiece. This is our home."

Janiece didn't say anything. She just knelt down and softly kissed her baby. She missed her like crazy, but she could imagine that Isaiah missed her more. She let him have her for what seemed like weeks when it had only been a few days. After she kissed her as softly as she could, they went back downstairs. She went to the kitchen, hoping he would have her favorite wine, and he did. After she grabbed a glass, he moved close to her from behind and then planted a kiss on her neck.

"I've been waiting forever to kiss your neck again."

"Isaiah, don't, okay? Please. I came so we could talk."

But he didn't stop. He continued to kiss her skin. "Jai, I missed you, baby, and I need you," he said, and she pulled away. "Why do you expect me to not want to touch you or kiss you? I haven't touched you in forever, and now you are back together with him, Janiece. I came home from war, and you act as if we are strangers. Why can't I touch you, babe? We were so good before I left. My only will to live came from thoughts of you and that little girl upstairs, and I have to come home and find out that the woman I fought to make it home to doesn't want me anymore," he cried.

The tears fell from her face as she heard his words. "Isaiah, I just can't. I have to go home."

"Janiece, this is your home," he yelled.

She swiped at her tears. This was going to be harder than she thought. She grabbed her glass and went out to the backyard. She sat, and she knew he'd come out to join her. He sat, and she looked at him. She hated that she was breaking his heart. He had already been through enough, but she had to tell him the truth. "Isaiah, this is so hard to say, but I am happy, and I know you didn't expect to come home to this, but this is what it is, and I don't know what you want me to do. I love you, but my love for K.P. grew all over again when I thought I had lost you. We are close, and I hate that I am breaking your heart, but I don't know what else to do. I can't be here and there at the same time."

"Janiece, I hear you, and I get everything, but tell me, what am I supposed to do? How do you think I feel? I never left you, we didn't break up, and my love for you got stronger every fucking minute that I survived that hell I was in. I was over there begging God to just let me get home to my girls, and now that He brought me out of the worst torment of my life, my happily ever after is gone. You just, boom, don't love me anymore. I can't accept that because what we had before I got on that fucking plane was real. I refuse to believe that we don't have a chance."

"I do love you, Isaiah, and this is hard for me too. I have literally fallen back in love with K.P., and I just don't know what to do. If I stay, I will break your heart. If I leave, I break his, Isaiah. This shit is not easy on me, either. We have this beautiful daughter, and I remember how bad I wanted us to have a family, and when you left,

I was miserable, and then I found out I was pregnant, and then I had hope, and then they showed up and said my husband was dead. I was on the verge of insanity, but K.P. came and helped me and had my back."

"I know and hear everything, and I am no fool, but I think that we still have something. If we don't spend time together, we won't get back to us, Jai. And you have to at least give us a shot before you just dead our shit. You married me first, so you can't just say fuck me and not even see if we can get back to where we were."

"What do you mean?"

"I mean, I want you to come home and give us a chance to see if we can get us back, and after a little time, if you don't want to continue with us, you can go back, and I will give you the divorce you want so you can legally marry K.P."

Janiece was still confused about what he was asking. "Please tell me what you are asking for."

"I mean, give us ninety days to see if you want to stay or go back. You move home, and for ninety days, we work on our marriage, and you give us a chance to rekindle our marriage. If, after ninety days, you want to go back to K.P. I will move on."

"Isaiah, K.P. is never going to go for that! That is crazy. K.P. will never go for that."

"Janiece, this has absolutely nothing to do with him. This is about us and saving our marriage. If you ever loved me, you'd give me that, at least. You have no idea what I've been through to make it back to you and Jaiden, and all I am asking is for ninety days to have my wife back and to see if we have something. Give me my chance to win you back because I love you so fucking much, and the last thing I ever wanted to come home to find out is that I lost you. Not just to K.P., but to any man. You're my wife, and every moment without you hurts me to the core," he expressed with tears in his eyes. "All I'm asking for is ninety days to see if you and I have a chance," he pleaded.

She didn't think his request was unreasonable, so she nodded and then said yes. He stood and then squatted in front of her and grabbed her hands and kissed them. She knew Isaiah loved her just as much as K.P. loved her, and she wondered how she would tell K.P. that she agreed to spend ninety days with Isaiah. He kissed her, and she allowed it. Their kiss became deeper, and she knew he was getting aroused.

"Let me make love to you?" he asked, and she froze.

"Isaiah, I can't," she protested.

"Janiece, it's been so long, baby. Please let me. I need you so bad," he pleaded, but she didn't stop him.

She screamed, *I can't do this,* on the inside, but this was Isaiah, and she knew he needed to release because she was sure he hadn't had any since the last time he had her. She let him kiss her down her neck, and he gave her a gentle nudge to lie back. He stood and stripped down to his boxer briefs. He went down on top of her, and he kissed her deeply. Her legs parted, and as soon as his dick pressed against her, he exploded. His body jerked, and Janiece was relieved but still couldn't believe that he had nutted.

"Isaiah did you just—"

"Yes, I did," he confessed, still breathing like he was out of breath. He got up, and she sat up. He headed inside, and a few minutes later, she went inside with him. Grateful he had on his boxers and didn't soil her dress, she followed him upstairs to get a towel to wipe off. She'd lose her panties because she wasn't walking into her house with Isaiah's fluids on her panties. She used the hall bathroom to wipe up. When she looked at her reflection, she just shook her head at herself. What in the hell was she doing? She didn't want to be in this love triangle again, and if she started fucking Isaiah, that was where she'd be all over again.

She left the washcloth on the sink, and she dropped her thong into the trash. When she got back to Isaiah, he was fully dressed with his head down. She took a seat. "I haven't since the last time when we . . ." he said.

"It's okay, and this was for the best, Isaiah. I don't want to be going back and forth between you and K.P. I mean, I love you two so much, and I just don't want to hurt anyone."

"Well, you are breaking my heart, and I just want you to consider what I asked."

"Isaiah, K.P. isn't going to agree to that."

"But do you agree with it?" he asked, and her mind said no, but her heart ached for him too.

"I'll talk to him, and I'll come back and give you what you are asking. You didn't leave me, so I can't imagine how much this hurts, and I want you to know that I do love you, Isaiah. Things are just not the same," she said, grabbing his hand.

He kissed the back of it. "I just want the chance to see if what we had can come back."

She nodded, and he stood and walked over to take the lid off the gas firepit. She again noticed that limp he now had. After he turned it on, he joined her again.

"Isaiah, what happened?"

"What do you mean?"

"You have a cane now, and you walk with a limp."

"War injury," was all he said and kept his eyes on the fire.

She stood. "I have to be going now."

"So soon?" he asked.

"Yes, I got to get home."

"Can you stay with me for a little while longer? Just let me hold you for a little while. I miss holding you close to me," he requested.

She contemplated it for a moment but couldn't say no. "Sure," she said.

"I'll refill your glass," he said and got her glass from the little table that sat between the lawn chairs. He went inside, and she took a seat. When he returned, he handed her the glass, and then she allowed him to sit on the chaise longue she occupied. She sipped, and they talked about the baby. And he asked a lot of questions, and soon, he reclined. She relaxed and lay in his arms, and she stayed for a couple of hours, and then she went to the bathroom. When she noticed the time, she went out to tell him she had to go.

"So when will you be back to our home?" he asked, looking up at her.

"Soon," she said and leaned in to kiss his lips. He walked her out and pulled her in for a tight hug. He didn't want to let her go, so she had to pull away. "Baby, I gotta go."

"I know, and I hope to see you back here soon," he said and then opened her door. She got in and cranked the engine. "I love you," he said.

"I love you too, Isaiah," she said, and he shut her door. She drove to the corner and stopped. She gripped the wheel and put her head against it and sobbed. What in the hell was she going to do? She loved them both. Before spending that little time with Isaiah, she was confident that she didn't want to go back, and now she didn't know. How could she choose one without hurting the other one? How could she choose K.P. when Isaiah went and damn near lost his life? How could she choose Isaiah when K.P. had been such a great husband to her? She sat there for damn near ten minutes until her phone rang. It was K.P.

She wiped her face and cleared her throat. "Hey, baby," she answered.

"What's up? I've been expecting you."

"I know, and I'm on my way now," she said, putting her car into gear.

"Okay," he said and paused. The line was quiet. "I love you, babe."

"I know, and I love you too, K.P. I'll be home real soon," she said and then ended the call. She blew out a breath and headed home.

Chapter Thirty-one

Janelle

When her phone alerted her that he was outside, she hurried out the door. Having him pick her up at home was risky, but since she hadn't seen Gregory in over a week, she figured, what the hell? They went to dinner, and it was nice, but Janelle couldn't help feeling guilty. She thought that seeing him again when she wanted to work out her marriage was a foolish choice. When he pulled up in her driveway, she decided to be honest and tell him how she felt.

"Thanks for dinner, Devon, I had a really nice time, but I have to be honest with you."

"What now? You have more kids you didn't tell me about?" he teased.

"No, nothing like that. It's just that I don't want to waste your time. I mean, going out with you was a great idea at first, but once we were seated, it hit me that I am not ready to date or see anyone. It would be best for us to leave this alone. I still love Greg, and it didn't hit me just how much I loved him until after he was gone. I miss you and have this serious attraction to you, that is a fact, but I want to be back with my husband until our marriage is resolved. I need to just sit my ass down somewhere, and I don't want to get all mixed up in my feelings again with you. It's not fair to you, because I want my husband back," she said.

"Okay, Janelle, I can understand that more than you know. I was the same with Leila. It really didn't hit me until after she was gone, so I respect your decision. Thank you for dinner, and don't lose my number. If someday you want to reach out and your situation is different, reach out. And I do hope that things work out for you and Gregory."

"Thanks, Devon, for being so understanding and not hating me for what I did."

"Nah. I was angry at first, but I've walked in your shoes, so I had to get over it."

"Thanks, and you take care of yourself. I wish the best for you too."

"Thanks. Have a good night," he said, and she gave Devon the last kiss that she'd ever share with him.

She walked inside, kicked off her shoes, and tossed her keys onto the counter. She hummed a tune from a song she heard earlier in the restaurant that reminded her of Gregory. She set the alarm and was all set to go upstairs, but she stopped in her tracks when she heard his voice.

"Where have you been?" he asked. The sound came from the family room. She hadn't even noticed him.

"Gregory, you scared the shit out of me. Why are you sitting in the damn dark?" She knew her sitter may have been in her guestroom sleeping because she told her she'd be late, and she volunteered to stay over.

"Waiting on you. Where in the hell have you been, and who dropped you off?"

"None of your business." She frowned.

"None of my business? You are my business."

"Since when? You don't give a damn about me, so what's with this third degree?"

"You were on a fucking date, Janelle, so tell me, what in the fuck is going on?" he said, getting in her face.

"Why are you asking me shit about what or who I'm doing, Gregory?"

"Because you are still my fucking wife!" he yelled.

"I'm tired, and I'm going to bed," Janelle said back through gritted teeth and then tried to walk away.

"Don't you walk away from me, Janelle! I want answers. Are you fucking him too?"

"Gregory, no! Not tonight. I'm not doing this shit with you tonight," she said and walked away.

"Fine, fuck it! I'm filing for a divorce," he announced, and she didn't argue. She wondered why he took so long to announce it when that was what he wanted.

"Fine, Gregory, go ahead and file. It's not like I expected anything different from you," she spat and tried to walk away.

"Janelle, don't you walk away from me. Do you have any fuckin' idea how many times that conversation with Devon plays in my mind? Him calling you 'baby' and informing me that you lied about our children and me? Do you have any idea how that shit feels?"

"No, Greg, I don't know how that feels because you shut me out. You don't talk to me, and you come and go like I'm a stranger. I am not a mind reader, so no, I have no idea what you are going through because you dipped out of here like you were waiting for a pass to go do what you wanna do, and I have no clue what you are feeling or going through because you shut me the fuck out! I have apologized and begged for you to come home and work our shit out for seven fuckin' months. You haven't made one effort to fix this or work it out, so if you want a damn divorce, just fuckin' file already because it is evident that you don't want me anymore," she threw at him. She thought he'd say something to defend himself, but instead, he grabbed her face and kissed her.

What the fuck? was her thought, but she didn't dare pull away. She needed his kiss and his touch, and his dick if they went that far. She missed her husband and missed her marriage, so when clothes were tugged away and thrown about, she did not protest. When she was laid back on the stairs and his lips and tongue connected with her nectar, she spread her limbs wider and moaned. She held his head and called out his name, and when she climaxed, he lapped up all of her juices. She had to give him a shove and a plea to have mercy for him to pull away.

When he took two steps up the stairs, they had gotten comfortable. His dick was harder than she remembered seeing in years, and she immediately grabbed him and put her mouth on him. She stroked and bobbed, making sure she allowed her throat to produce the most saliva that would give him a sloppy experience. He groaned as she pleased him and then grabbed a handful of her curls. He coached her with words of affirmation that she was getting the job done, and that encouraged her to deep throat him like a champion. She gagged, but the amount of saliva her throat produced only enhanced the experience, and when he snatched away and held on to his rod like he was protecting it from an eruption, she knew it was time to let him inside of her again.

She lay back on the stairs and spread her legs wide again, and he got into a push-up position on top of her. She was wet, ready, and so turned on, but her core hadn't had him in months, so it stung like a bitch. She gasped, panted, and squealed as he opened her up again. She hadn't expected that level of discomfort, and when he glided in and out, she whimpered. She knew it was all good for him because his groans and, "Ahhh shit, baby," echoed in their lower level.

She allowed the painful thrusts because his groans sounded more like anger than pain. She knew she had hurt him, and he was depositing all of his pain inside of her with every painful stroke.

"Baby, please, take it easy," she tried to say, but he continued to drive his dick in and out of her like he was finally letting go of all the pain he had been carrying around the last few months. She squealed and endured the rough and aggressive strokes that he delivered with his occasional nipple suck. He came down to her, and she wrapped her arms and legs around him, and he slowed. He then gave her a slow roll, and his body trembled, and she heard him cry. He cried and stroked, and he groaned out loud when he climaxed.

His weight rested on her, and he was heavy. Her back was pressed against the stairs, but she just endured it. After what seemed like an eternity, he rolled off of her. He wiped his eyes, and she softly touched his back. "I'm so sorry for hurting you, baby. I swear, I wish I could take it all back."

"I know," he said and then got up. He walked down a few steps and went for his clothes and began to dress.

"You're not staying?"

"No."

"Why not?" she asked, confused. They had just made love again after seven-plus months, and his leaving didn't make any sense.

"Because this doesn't mean we're getting back to-gether," he declared, and her eyes watered. That stung because she was certain that he would try after what just went down.

"What the fuck, Greg, what was this about? You fucking with my emotions?"

"No."

"Then what the fuck is it? What do you want from me?"

"I want for you to have never ridden another man's dick," he said and finished dressing.

There were no more words exchanged, and when he left, Janelle sobbed on the stairs. She was angry at him and at herself, and she declared that she would let his ass go and move the fuck on with her life.

Chapter Thirty-two

Janiece

She walked in and tried to hurry by him. He was on the sofa watching the nature channel, she guessed, because she saw elephants on the screen.

"Hey, babe," he said.

"Hey," she said and tried to keep moving.

"Jai, come here," he said, sitting up.

She paused and turned to him. She didn't want to go anywhere near him until she brushed her teeth and washed away Isaiah's touch from her skin. She didn't even want him to smell the lingering scent of his cologne that clung to her body and clothes.

"What is it, babe? I need to use the bathroom," she said nervously.

"Oh, okay, it's just odd for you to walk in and not greet me with a kiss," he said, standing and moving toward her.

"Can we talk after I go to the bathroom?" she asked, backing away.

"Sure," he said, and she hurried off.

When she got into their master bathroom, she stripped and started the shower. She tinkled and brushed her teeth and gargled before stepping in. When she got out, she put on her robe, and when she opened the door, K.P. was right there sitting on the bench at the foot of their bed with his eyes locked on her.

"What happened?" he asked.

"What do you mean?" she said, sliding her hands into the pockets of her robe.

"Exactly what I said. What happened at Isaiah's? Did you fuck him?"

"No, K.P., no. Why would you ask me something like that?"

"I don't know. You rushed up in here and went straight to the shower and shit, so tell me what happened."

"Okay, I'll tell you the truth, K.P.," she said and lowered her head. She looked down at the pink polish on her toes, searching for the words to say what she had to say.

"Are you going to tell me now?" he asked.

She looked at him and then cleared her throat. "I didn't have sex with him, but I was going to," she confessed, and he was up and in her face within seconds.

"Say that shit again," he said.

"Look, I need you to sit and just listen, please," she said, and he didn't budge. "K.P., please, sit. I promised to always be honest with you, and this is not the time to start lying to you, so sit down and let me explain it all."

He gave her a look of fear as opposed to anger. He looked terrified to even hear what she had to say to him, but he sat back down on the bench. "Okay, explain," he said with his eyes locked dead on hers.

"First, we did kiss, and the kiss turned into a passionate one, and things were getting heated. I tried to shut it down, but Isaiah missed me and he loves me, and I felt like I owed it to him. I don't know, but after the next kiss, I didn't fight it, but it was over before it started because he hadn't touched a woman since our last time. You know, before we even did anything," she said, and he just stared at her. "I'm sorry that this is where we are right now, but I can't lie to you."

"I had a feeling that you would. I am relieved that it didn't happen, but I can't say that I'm thrilled to hear this shit, Janiece. I mean, what is going to happen now? What is the real story? Are you going to go back to him now?"

"Yes," she said, and K.P. looked at her as if she were a stranger.

"What?"

"I agreed to go back," she said, and he jumped up.

"What the fuck, Janiece? Are you just going to leave me now? After how far we have finally come, you are just going to fucking leave me?" he yelled.

"K.P., please, wait a minute and listen to what I have to say. Just please sit down and let me explain."

"Explain what, Janiece? You come home and hit me with this. What's to explain?" he blasted.

"Kerry, please lower your voice and listen to me. Please," she said gently, putting her hand on his chest. "I love you, and I'm not leaving for good. At least, I don't think I am. Just hear me out."

"What are you saying?"

"Just sit, please, and let me tell you."

He hesitated but eventually sat.

She took a deep breath and cleared her throat. "I agreed to go back for ninety days," she said, and when he didn't interrupt, she continued. The way his brows knitted together, she knew he was as confused as she was when Isaiah asked her. "Isaiah won't give me a divorce unless I give him a fair chance to see if we still have something."

"That's crazy, Janiece. We are married. We got married," he restated.

"Technically, according the State of Illinois, I am still married to him. I am still his wife, and Isaiah showed me all this proof that I'd have to divorce him in order for our marriage to be legal. So he asked me to give him ninety days to see if I want to truly be done."

"And you think giving your ex another chance is a brilliant idea?"

"Yes, I do because I owe him that, K.P. Can you please just look beyond the norm and understand how hard all of this really is for me? Isaiah didn't leave me, divorce me, or break up with me. He got on a damn plane to go and fight for this country and ended up being a POW, and I can't imagine what they put him through, and he comes back to this," she said, waving her arms in the air. "His wife is back with the very same man he was in the same situation before a few years ago. For once, think of what Isaiah is going through."

"Wow," he said and laughed a little. "You still love him."

"I do, and I still love you. This is the craziest thing to have to ask you, and I can't imagine how hard this is. It's a bitch on us all, but I have to give him ninety days, just like I would give you if it were you instead of him. I need this because I don't want to live with days of what-ifs or resent you," she said, and tears welled in her eyes.

"I need you to understand that I love both of you so much. I need to try to rekindle this thing with him to make sure who I want to be with. I'd give my right hand not to be in this situation right now with the two men I know who to love me so much. Some would think I got it good, but I don't, because if I stay, I break his heart. If I go, I'll break yours, and I'm not going back to him for him. I'm going back for me because I have to be sure I'm here if I'm here or there if I'm there," she cried, hoping he'd understand.

He stood and wrapped his arms around her. She sobbed, and he held her and then said, "How can I agree to let you go? I love you, Jai."

"And I love you too, K.P., and even if you don't agree, I'm going. I have to give him what he is asking. He deserves it."

"What am I supposed to do for ninety days while you are there?"

"Just wait for me."

"Jai," he released, shaking his head.

"Do you love me enough to wait for me, Kerry?"

He just stared her in the eyes for a few moments and then replied, "I do, and at this point, you are going to go even if I don't agree, so okay." He released her and walked out of the room.

She fell onto the bench and sobbed. She didn't want to go, and if she stayed, she'd never know if she and Isaiah could get back to where they were before he deployed. She cried until her head ached. She climbed into bed after she put on her nightgown.

K.P. finally came to bed, and he moved in close to her. He began to caress her skin, and then she turned onto her back. He kissed her passionately, and that night he made love to Janiece like it would be his last time. The passion was intensified. She had three orgasms, and he had two before he finally tumbled onto the bed beside her. They were quiet after they finally stopped panting like animals.

K.P. broke the silence. "What if you don't come back to me, Jai?" he asked in the dark.

"What if I do?"

"Again, what if you don't?"

"That will mean that I did you a favor of leaving you instead of staying when I knew I wanted to be with another man. That will mean that I'm not sneaking around and fucking around with my daughter's dad because there's just something about him I can't get over. You don't see it right now, but whether I come back or I don't, it will be the best for you."

"How so? I can't see that you not coming back would be a benefit for me."

"It would be because it would give you the true freedom to find love again. I just want to give you and Isaiah the freedom to have a chance whether I'm there or not. You may not ever understand, but I just need you to promise me that if or when I come back, you can love me and not ask about any details or play-by-plays of my time with him. If or when I come back, I want you to just move forward with me."

"Given the fact that I'd never want to hear the details of what you will or won't be doing when you are with him, my answer is I promise." With that, they cuddled close and slept skin to skin.

Over the next few days, they acted like they always did, and it was natural to Janiece. She just concentrated on K.P. and focused on them. Leaving day was melancholy, and they didn't exchange many words. He walked her out, and after she was in her car, she cranked the engine and let her window down. "Keep these safe for me," she said, handing him her wedding rings. The set that Isaiah had given her was in her purse, and she planned to put them back on.

"Janiece, I'd do anything for you," he said, and she believed him. As crazy as their history was, she knew K.P. truly loved her.

"I know, baby, and I love you," she said. He leaned in and kissed her lips one last time. He finally let her hand go. She reminded him to not call her at any time unless it was dire. She rolled away, and she wiped tears from her face the entire ride.

Chapter Thirty-three

Janiece

When Janiece walked in, Isaiah rushed to her and pulled her into his arms. "Welcome home, baby," he cheered and gave her a wet kiss on the lips. Jaiden entered the living room, and Janiece was so happy to see her baby. When Isaiah released her, she scooped her up and gave her a ton of kisses. Isaiah then wrapped his arms around the both of them. He held them for what felt like an eternity before he let them go. He unloaded Janiece's things from the car and took them up to the master. Janiece went up to settle in while he made dinner.

"Baby, dinner is ready," he yelled up the stairs. Janiece was just about finished unpacking and putting her things away.

"I'll be down in a minute," she yelled back. She took her last couple of clothes on hangers into their walk-in, and then she noticed two pillows and a couple of blankets on the floor against the wall and wondered why they were in the closet and not the other linen closet. She shook it off because it wasn't important and headed downstairs. The baby was already in her high chair, and she could tell they were waiting for her. "I'm sorry, baby. I was just trying to finish it all before I ate and got lazy," she said with a smile. It was nice to be back home with him. They chose that home together, and he managed to have it set up just the way she had set it up.

During dinner, Isaiah had her laughing, reminiscing about their past. He reminded her of so many fun times, and when they cleared the table, they danced and sang like they used to, and Janiece decided to just enjoy it. She'd give it a real chance and see if she could love him as deeply as she had before.

After dinner, they continued to catch up until it was time to bathe Jaiden. They did that together for the first time and kept smiling at each other. After they put the baby down, they went back to the sofa.

"The entire time I was over there, this was all I dreamed of doing," he said, breaking the silence. They had been in a staring and smiling state since they had sat. "This is finally my reality, and having my family here in this house makes me so happy right now, Janiece. I can't say how much this entire day has felt like a dream," he said and stood. He reached out his hand, "Let's sit outside." She took his hand, and they made a pit stop in the kitchen. She poured her favorite wine, and he fixed his favorite brown liquor.

This was light at first until Isaiah asked her, "What made you go back to him?"

"What?" she asked because he said it so low.

"What made you go back to K.P. of all the men on this planet? You went back to him and pretty quickly, according to my sister and dad," he added.

Janiece let out an annoyed sigh. "You are kidding me, right?"

"What?"

"Your evil sister and your father treated me like the help when you died," she said, catching herself. "I'm sorry, babe, I just meant after we thought you died, I was a wreck, and K.P. just showed up at that right moment, and that right moment was the worst moment for your family, and things just spiraled from then," she shared. She told Isaiah everything, the entire truth, and he was mad as hell.

"I'm so sorry that you had to go through that. I mean, they've convinced me of all these other things that now make no sense because, from what you've told me, they left you no choice."

"It was difficult losing you. I have something for you."

"What you got?" he joked.

"Hold on," she got up and went inside to get her iPad. She came back and told him to sit closer. She tapped a few buttons and went to her photos and videos. "Since you didn't get to be here for the pregnancy, I have over two dozen videos and hundreds of pictures for you to see what you've missed. I'm going to go and shower and let you enjoy," she said and gave him a kiss. She headed inside and went up to shower.

When she walked away, he focused on the tons of pictures and videos. He just tapped the screen and scrolled. He enjoyed picture after picture and video after video. There were pics and videos from before his daughter was born, and he kept scrolling until he landed on one where his wife was in a gown that he didn't recognize. It immediately started to play, and his finger hovered over it to bypass it, but he just listened.

"Well, baby, today is the day. I never thought I'd be doing this again because when I married you, I married my forever, but I guess God needed you more there with Him than I needed you here with me. I do miss you every day and all day, and you're probably up there like, 'K.P. of all people?' and yeah, K.P. He loves me, Isaiah, the way you did, and I feel that. He is going to be good to me and take care of me, and I know in my heart that that is what you'd want for me. You loved me unselfishly, so I believe in my heart that you are up there happy for me. I will honestly tell you that this is the happiest I've been since you've been gone, baby. Listen, they are knocking for me now, so I gotta go. Wish me luck, and I'll never forget you, and I'll never stop loving you," she said and blew a kiss at the camera.

By the end, his eyes were wet. After everything she had told him about her experience with his family and how beautiful she looked on her wedding day, he then understood why K.P. had won her heart again.

He just had to figure out how to win it back. The story of what she went through and the videos, some happy, a lot sad from when he was away and the ones after she thought he was dead, gave him clarity about why it was K.P., and he wasn't so angry about it anymore. He saw the ones with her crying her eyes out for how his family was treating her and how they treated her after Jaiden was born.

His only focus was reconnecting with his wife and hoping that, after ninety days, she'd be home to stay. When he finished the last video, he headed inside. He wondered why Janiece hadn't returned. When he made it to the bedroom, she was rubbing lotion on her skin in a white tank and a thong. Immediately his dick stiffened, and he grabbed it.

"Let me help you," he said quickly, moving across the room.

"Thanks, baby," she said, handing over the bottle, and she kissed his lips back when he kissed hers.

"Please don't say no tonight. I really need you," he said.

"I know, and I won't. I know what you need and want," she answered as he rubbed lotion on her ass cheeks. He finished moisturizing her skin and pulled her into her arms. They kissed deeply, and then he pulled away.

"Let me shower, Jai."

"Okay," she said and gave him another peck. He went to shower, and she went to check on their sleeping daughter.

Chapter Thirty-four

Janiece

She climbed into bed and tried so hard to stop thinking of K.P. She missed his voice, and she wanted to call him so bad. She was having a great time with Isaiah, and it was nice, but K.P. stayed in her thoughts. That night Isaiah limped into their room, she looked at his body, and she was still attracted to and turned on by him. He had gotten bigger, meaning even more muscular than he was, and even with a limp and a couple of missing toes, he was still fine as hell. She paused their kiss and went down for a glass of wine. Before she headed back up, he appeared in the kitchen wearing long shorts and a tank.

"What's taking you so long, baby?"

"I just came for wine," she said, holding up the glass.

"Can you also cum for me?" he asked, moving over to her. She fell back onto the stool that sat behind her. He moved in between her legs.

"Oh, that's what you came down here to do?"

"Nah, but I can. Just let me put you on this island," he said, swiftly hoisting her onto the island. "You know something?"

"No, what?" she asked, wrapping her arms around his neck.

"When we moved here, we fucked in every room, even the walk-in closet, but never here in the kitchen," he said and kissed her.

"You are right," she said in between pecks.

"I used to have this dream of you sucking my dick in this kitchen," he said, and her eyes went wide at his words.

"So again, you want that dream to come true?" she said, teasing his tongue with hers.

"Oh, yes, I do," he said, moving her hand to his erection.

That was one thing that war did not take from her husband, his big-ass dick. She slid down and went into her famous squat. She went all in, giving Isaiah the "welcome home" head that he deserved, and that night there was no minute-man action. She didn't know if he had been jerking off to be back to normal, but he was back, and the lovemaking was just as good as it had been before he left.

By the time her head hit the pillow, the thoughts of what just went down with Isaiah had escaped her mind. As good as it all physically felt to her body, it still didn't satisfy her emotions and heart. She tried to brush off the thoughts of K.P. as she reminded herself that it was only day one. Isaiah had eighty-nine more days to rejuvenate their marriage.

The next morning, Isaiah made breakfast, and they had a great day. They spent time with their daughter and just did what they used to do. The days moved by fast, and Janiece was still torn, but not because she wasn't figuring out where she truly wanted to be. She was just sad because she knew she would break his heart. She knew that there would be no happy ending for him, and she cringed at the calendar because the days rolled by fast sometimes and dragged others.

Janiece woke from a deep sleep around five in the morning. She was used to waking at eight or nine with him not being there because he was a soldier. She knew he was an early riser. She relieved her bladder first and went to find her husband. She checked the baby's room first, and no Isaiah. She went downstairs, and he wasn't there, and both cars were in their drive. She opened the basement door, and it was pitch-black, so she knew he wasn't down there. She went back to their room, and then she heard soft snores coming from the closet. She eased over to the door and then opened it to find him sleeping. She was afraid to touch him, but she had to wake him.

"Isaiah, baby," she whispered, but he didn't stir. She contemplated whether to wake him. She didn't want to be tackled by him. She recalled waking him one time before, and he woke up like he was going to hurt her. She went on to her knees and tugged the covers, and when he moved, his left foot was exposed. She jumped because she had never paid close attention to his foot since the accident. She covered her mouth and suppressed her urge to cry. She took a few breaths and pulled away his covers. He was shirtless, something he hadn't been since he came home. They made love with his chest and back in a tank or tee every time, and now she saw all of his battle scars. She then crawled into the closet with him and snuggled close to him.

She knew he felt her presence when he said, "I wanted to tell you."

"Why?" she asked, and he knew her and what she was asking.

"I just can't get comfortable in that bed. I've tried, but I can't," he answered.

"What did they do to you, Isaiah? I saw the scars, baby, and they are horrible." She sniffled. Now she was crying.

"Nothing that I would want to tell you about, Jai," was his response. "The important thing is I'm home now, and all that is behind me."

"We can shop for a firmer mattress. The pillow top can go," she said. "We can even get a low platform bed. I just want you close to me every night, all night," she said.

"I'm not crazy, baby. A little traumatized, but I'm not crazy."

She turned over to face him. "No, baby, don't say shit like that. I don't think that at all. I just want to help. Please don't think I think that."

"Okay, anyway, I'm doing everything I'm supposed to do. I don't miss any appointments, and I do everything I'm supposed to do because I have you and li'l Jai, and I will do whatever for my family," he said.

"I know," she said and relaxed in his arms. "And I'm so sorry that after all you've gone through, you had to come home to me and—"

"Don't say his name," he said sternly. "These ninety days are about us and our marriage and our everything. He . . ." He paused. "Just don't say his name. Whatever you decide at the end is what you decide, Janiece, and I am cherishing our time."

She didn't say anything more. She just dozed off. A couple of hours later, she heard her baby crying and yelling, "Momma, Momma, Momma," and "Da, Da, Da," at the top of her lungs. Janiece jumped up, and she realized they were in the closet with the door closed, and Jaiden had to be looking for them. She hurried out and went and picked her baby up to comfort her. Her face was drenched with tears, and she was talking baby talk, and Janiece imagined she was explaining how scared she was looking for them. Janiece carried her to the master bathroom and sat her on the vanity while she peed. Isaiah walked in, and the baby reached for him, and he picked her up.

"Why the sad face, pumpkin?" he asked.

"We were in the closet, and she couldn't find us."

"Oh, wow, I bet she was terrified. I guess we need a new bed, and I got to get better," he said and planted a kiss on the baby's cheek.

"True and true, and you will."

"I know," he replied, and even though Janiece was still sitting on the toilet, he kissed her forehead. "I'm going to head down to make breakfast," he announced, and he and the baby vacated the bathroom.

"I'll be down shortly to help," she said to his back.

By the time she made it down, he was cooking and had the phone on speaker. Something was going on with his parents that evening, and he assured his mother they'd be there. Janiece wanted to tell him to go without her because his family hated her, but she remembered that she agreed to give 100 percent to this, so later that afternoon, she rode to her in-laws with a fake smile on her face to not remove the big smile on Isaiah's face.

Chapter Thirty-five

Janiece

She rode in silence while Isaiah and Jaiden sang along with the tunes from the radio. Her little voice trying to sing the words made Janiece smile, which made him smile at her. She took his hand and gave it a gentle squeeze. She turned back to look out the window and wished she could just focus on them, but thoughts of K.P. often danced around her mind. She missed him and just wanted to see him. She'd browse his photos on her phone or listen to old messages on her phone just to hear his voice. She wanted to just forget him and recommit to Isaiah, but she was having difficulty with it.

She didn't want to get out of the car when they parked. "What are all these cars doing here?"

"I don't know. This was supposed to be dinner."

"Looks more like a party, and I'm so not in the mood for this, Isaiah. You know how your family feels about me."

"It doesn't matter what they think. I love you. That's all that matters," he said and got the baby from her car seat. They walked in holding hands, and the evil eyes darted at Janiece.

"Hey, big bro," Iyeshia said and just addressed Janiece. "I didn't know you were coming," she said after erasing the smile she gave her brother.

"Why wouldn't my wife come, Iyeshia?"

"Well, I just thought she was still hoing with that other nigga," she said.

"Well, you thought wrong, and watch yo' mouth," he said, pulling Janiece toward the backyard. He went looking for his parents. They exchanged greetings, and his mother immediately took Jaiden out of his arms. There were plenty of family and friends and too many women hugging her husband too tight and too long. Although her husband had a limp and sometimes used his cane, he was still fine. His chocolate skin glowed in the sun, and his slanted eyes were even sexy when he squinted. His smile was gorgeous, and Janiece learned that he had veneers now. She kept a close eye on him because this one female wouldn't keep her damn distance. Janiece decided to introduce herself as his wife so she could move the fuck around the yard.

She managed to have a good day at the Lawtons'. Aside from Iyeshia's digs, things went well. After the crowd had finally cleared out, Janiece was helping Isaiah's mom in the kitchen. Iyeshia had taken Jaiden upstairs to try to get her to sleep, so it was just the two of them.

"So how are things, Janiece?"

"Fine, everything is great."

Doreen raised a brow and dug into their business. "Listen, Janiece, you don't have to pretend with me. I love my son to death, and I know this is difficult for you."

"No, ma'am, I love Isaiah," she defended herself.

"Yes, and I've seen the way you look at K.P. as opposed to the way you look at my son. You don't have to say anything out loud, but be true to Isaiah and yourself. My son's ninety-day rekindle idea was crazy, and I told him to just move on, but he loves you so much that moving on wasn't an option for him. But woman to woman," she said, taking Janiece by her hands and looking her in her eyes, "I am sure there was a time when you loved him as deeply as he loves you, I won't deny that, but things are different now. You have made decisions that you can't come back from. All I'm asking you to do is what's best for you both when it's all said and done. If you want to return to K.P., let my son be free to find love again.

"It would be a terrible thing to long for another man while staying with someone your heart truly doesn't want. Life is too short for all of the games and lies. Don't let guilt or pity be the reason you stay. That wouldn't make either of you happy in the long run. However, if you decided to stay, just love my son with everything and give me more beautiful grandkids to spoil and love."

Tears welled in Janiece's eyes, and she nodded. "Yes, ma'am, I understand," she said and hugged her tight. "Thank you for saying that. Since my mother is gone, you are the closest thing to a mom to me, so thank you for never judging me and for not hating me for my choices. I would have never left him if he hadn't gone over there," she explained, and she released her to look at her face. "I never cheated on Isaiah while we were married. Not with K.P. or any other man, I swear on my life," she cried.

"I know, Janiece," she said, and then Iyeshia walked in.

"Where did Daddy and Saiah go, Ma?" she asked.

"Out back," Doreen said, giving a point.

Iyeshia gave Janiece a quick eye roll even though she saw her wiping away tears. Janiece knew she hated her being there. Janiece got back to helping her mother-in-law, and Iyeshia headed out the back door.

Chapter Thirty-six

Isaiah

"Daddy, can I have a word with Saiah for a moment?" Iyeshia asked.

"Sure, sure," he said and got up. He laid a hand on Isaiah's shoulder. "Again, I'm so proud of you, son, and if she makes you happy, she makes you happy," his dad said because he had just talked with his son about taking Janiece back after what she had done.

He was so tired of people telling him what to do about his wife, and he figured that Iyeshia wanted the same conversation. He had avoided his family since Janiece came home, and he didn't expect anything different from them.

"What's up, sis?" he asked.

"Saiah, really, you bring her up in here? How could you take her back after all the shit she has done to you?" she spat, damn near yelling.

"Iesh, calm down and stop it with this shit. I know you can't stand her, and we can live with that, but you will stop disrespecting her."

"Isaiah, she is a tramp-ass bitch!" she blasted.

"Iyeshia," he yelled, "I'm so fucking sick and tired of this bullshit and this feud you have with my wife. Janiece is not perfect, and she did something that no one likes, but my wife ain't no tramp bitch, so watch yo' fucking mouth," he yelled at her, something he had never done. Well, not like that.

"I've been telling you since the New Year's Eve episode to leave her, and you just can't see that she is stuck on that dude. As soon as your casket went into the ground, he showed up, and she ran right back to him, Isaiah. That disrespectful muthafucka had the nerve to show up there," she spat, and he knew she was pissed about that, but that was old news. "What kinda spell does that trick have on you, big bro?"

"Okay, Iesh, enough with the name-calling. That shit stops now! You want to be real, let's be real. Let's do it! You've had it in for her since something that went down years ago, and I married her. She chose me, remember? Aside from all that shit, I'm a grown-ass man, and I will be with who the fuck I want to be with. This 'hate Isaiah's girl' has been your thing since I started dating, and you need to get some damn business of your own and stay out of mine. And y'all pretty much pushed her back into K.P.'s arms."

"What! You blame us for that . . ." She paused. Isaiah knew she was about to call her a name, but she continued. "You are trying to say we're to blame for her returning to him?"

"That is exactly what the fuck I am saying. My wife was pregnant with my daughter, and y'all tossed her out of our home, Iyeshia. Tell me, is that bullshit being there for a pregnant, grieving wife? Y'all not only kicked her out of our house, y'all demanded a test on my damn daughter, treating my wife like a lying whore. And even when y'all got confirmation that Jaiden was mine, you didn't give her a dime and had the audacity to take sole custody of the only part of me that my wife had left. So I don't blame her for running back to the only person who was there for her when her in-laws put her through hell. K.P. isn't my favorite person, but he was there for the two people I love the most, and that's more than I can say for you and Dad.

"After she told me how y'all treated her and all the disrespect and name-calling, I was disgusted by acting crazy with her in front of my child. So if you hate Janiece, tough. She is my wife, and you don't have to ever say shit to my wife! I've let you destroy relationships with women in the past because no one has ever been good enough for your brother. That shit stops today. I don't need your damn opinion or permission to be with anyone. I love you, sis, but if you can't accept my wife, we will forever be at odds because I'm not leaving her," he said and stood. He limped away, leaving his sister sitting there with tears in her eyes.

"Jai, get Jaiden so we can go," he ordered, and both Janiece and his mom looked at him.

"Baby, what's wrong?" Janiece asked.

"Just get our daughter!" he yelled, but then he corrected himself. "I didn't mean to yell, Jai, and I'm sorry, but can you please just get the baby?"

She gave a quick nod and went for the stairs. With the commotion, his father walked into the kitchen.

"What in the world is going on?" he asked as Iyeshia walked through the back door.

"Listen," he said, addressing everyone in the kitchen, "I know how y'all treated my wife, and she asked me to never mention it and to just let it go, and at first I was going to, but tonight changed that. Y'all kicked my pregnant wife out and treated her like an outcast. No one respected her decisions to ensure that she and my unborn child would be okay. Y'all drove my wife back to this man and treated her like a harlot. If y'all would have supported her, been there for her, and helped her, maybe

I would have come home to a different scenario."

"Son, we did what we thought was best," his dad stated.

"Y'all tested my daughter, Dad. Really?" he said. Then Janiece walked in with the baby and her bag. "Look, y'all don't have to love her or even like her, but this is my wife, and if y'all want to continue to see Jaiden and me, y'all will show some damn respect to her. If y'all can't, Dad and Iyeshia," he called out because he knew his mother didn't feel the same way, but he was disappointed that she didn't do shit to stop it, "I won't be coming around."

"Babe, don't say that," Janiece said.

"No, I am dead serious," he declared, taking his daughter from Janiece's arms. He grabbed her hand and led her to the door. They didn't even say bye. They just walked out the door.

"Are you okay?" she asked him after she fastened her seat belt.

"I'm good, and from now on, I'll never let them hurt or disrespect you."

She gave him a half-smile and a nod. "Isaiah, I do love you. I do," she said, and her eyes glossed over.

"I know you do, and we're going to be okay, baby," he said, and they kissed. He cranked the car, and they rode home in silence, holding hands.

Chapter Thirty-seven

Kerry

"Are you all right, man?" Marcus asked him and then took a sip of his Crown.

"No, I'm not. You know damn well I'm not okay, damn. My wife has been with her other husband for ninety damn days, and Sunday, I'll know if she is coming back to me or staying with him."

"Damn, that time went by fast."

"No, the fuck it didn't."

"Of course not for you, but since you told me that crazy-ass idea it seems as though it flew by."

"For the kids and me, it was long and hard."

"Why are you so worried? You and Janiece got history, and y'all are meant for each other. I say relax. She'll be back. She loves you."

"Man, I just don't feel confident. She and Isaiah were tight, and she chose him once, so I can't say she won't again. They have a daughter together, and I'm terrified, Marcus."

"I wouldn't have let her go back," Marcus said, shaking his head.

"I had to. This was what she needed, so it wasn't about me. If I had fought her, she would have still returned to him. She loves him just as much as she loves me, and that sounds strange as hell saying it out loud, but it is just the damn truth."

"What will you do if she decides to stay with Isaiah?"

He hunched his shoulders. "Let go. I mean, what choice would I have? She can't be with us both, and if I can't have her back faithful and true to me, I don't need her. I want her to be happy at the end of the day, but it will break my heart."

"Man, this is definitely the craziest shit I've heard in my life, but I'm rooting for you, and I hope she comes home on Sunday."

"Me too, man, me too."

Chapter Thirty-eight

Janelle

"Hey, sis," Janelle said when her sister walked in.

"Hey, girlie," she said and gave her a peck on the cheek. She put her purse down and took a seat at the island.

"So it's decision weekend, huh?" she said, getting two wineglasses.

"It is."

"Annnndddddd?"

"I'm not telling you because I'm still going to take the weekend to be certain this is what I really want."

"Damn, no hint," she said, pouring the red wine into the glasses.

"Nope, and where are the kids?"

"At Greg's parents'. They are taking them to *SpongeBob* or somebody on ice, and I am going to have my weekend alone to just pamper myself." She smiled, handing Janiece a glass.

"As you should," she said and held up her glass. They tapped and sipped. "What is the latest on Gregory?"

"He finally sent the papers. I haven't signed them yet, but I will. I can't make it work alone, so it is what it is."

"I'm sorry, sis. I know you still love him."

"More than he knows, but I fucked up."

"Yes, well, at least you don't have to break a man's heart on Sunday."

"True, and I can't imagine how hard that is."

"Janelle, it is the worst. I love both of them so much for so many different reasons, and I know both would do whatever it takes to make me happy, so Sunday, I will live with my decision."

"As long as you are happy, K.P. or Isaiah will be all right."

"I know, but this shit is painful as hell."

"I can't imagine, and I've decided not to mope around this house. I am moving forward with my life and accepting what it is."

"Well, you are looking good, back down to the size you were before the twins. Skin glowing and curls popping, you will meet someone else."

"I know, but I'm not even thinking about another man right now. I just want to do me for a while."

"What's up with Devon?" she asked.

"I don't know. Haven't talked to him since the last time I saw him."

"Do you want to see him?"

"Nah, that was a part of my problem and needs to stay dead."

"I hear ya," Janiece said and polished off her glass. She stood. "Well, I'm going to go check into my room, pamper myself, and go home to my husband on Sunday."

"Which husband is that?" Janelle tried again.

"The one I choose," Jai playfully answered.

They hugged, and Janelle walked her sister out. She locked up, made a reservation for her favorite restaurant, and then hung around her empty house that afternoon, not doing much of anything. Around six, she dressed and headed out to dinner. When she arrived and was seated, she was proud that she was dining alone and not too afraid to be seen eating by herself.

The server approached, and she ordered a white wine. She took a sip of the water that sat on her table. She looked over the menu, although she already knew what she'd order, and when she casually scanned the restaurant, she noticed that no one else was dining alone. She felt a little uncomfortable for a moment, but after her order was in and a few sips of her wine, she was relaxed and happy that she had come out. She nibbled on the bread, sipped, and looked around the restaurant again.

Her eyes landed on her husband pulling out a chair for a woman. She blinked to ensure it was Greg, and it was definitely him. She took a closer look at the woman and recognized her from Hotel Dana. Janelle tried to stay calm, but her hands began to tremble.

She was alone when he was with a beautiful woman, which made her feel even worse. She drained her wine and signaled for her server. She had to get the hell out of there. He hurried over, and she asked for her bill.

"But, ma'am, you haven't gotten your meal yet."

"I know, but there was an emergency, and I have to go, so please hurry," she said, hoping that Greg wouldn't see her.

"Do you want your meal to go?" he politely offered.

"No, just get my ticket now, please." She gave him her card, and when he came back, she signed and stood. It hit her that she had to walk by his table to leave unless she went through the kitchen behind her.

"Fuck," she mumbled and then just decided to speak and then make her exit just in case he noticed her.

"Gregory, I thought that was you. How are you?" she said, doing a horrible job playing cool. She visibly shook because she was so angry, nervous, and pissed.

He looked up at her, and she wanted to disappear. "I'm well, and it's good to see you," he said, and she knew he was lying.

She looked at the gorgeous woman. "Forgive the interruption. I'm Janelle, an old friend of Gregory's."

The woman seemed unbothered. "It's fine, no worries. I'm Kelley Michelson," she replied.

At that moment, Janelle was starting to come undone, and she felt her eyes burning. "Nice to meet you, Kelley, and you two enjoy," she said and hurried to get as far away from their table as possible.

"Janelle," she heard him call out when he stepped outside the restaurant.

At that point, she was already standing outside of the building sobbing. She heard her name again, and then he was closer, but she kept her back to him. He approached, and then she felt him embrace her from the back.

"That is business. Nothing is going on," he said.

"It doesn't matter, Greg, and I'm sorry for even stopping by your table."

He turned her to face him and lifted her head by her chin. "I'm not sleeping with her, and I never have."

"It doesn't matter. I messed everything up by cheating and ruined our marriage, so even if you are, it doesn't matter."

"I was an asshole," he said.

Her brows bunched together because she was confused by his response. She was the one who had cheated. She may have felt that he was cheating, but she never had any proof like he had on her. "No, Greg, it was me," she tried to say, but he cut her off with a kiss.

Shocked again, she was not in the mood to play these games with Gregory, so she pulled away. "No, stop, Greg. This is insane. You have a date waiting for you."

"You need to come with me," he ordered, pulling her by the hand.

"Wait, please stop. I'm embarrassed enough. What are you doing?"

"Something I should have done long ago. Now trust me for once."

She didn't know what he was up to, but she followed him back inside. He stopped an employee walking back and asked for him to bring a third chair to his table. They approached the table, and the woman looked up.

"Kelley, I'm sorry for all the confusion. I want to formally introduce you to my lovely wife, Janelle Peoples. She was out having dinner alone because her husband was a major ass, and he was foolish, and if you don't mind, I'd like for her to join us."

"No, I certainly don't mind. We can quickly get the signatures done and enjoy dinner."

Janelle was stunned and overwhelmed with joy. "Let me just go to the ladies' room," she said. She had to go freshen up.

"Of course," Greg said.

She hurried to the ladies' room and got herself back together. By the time she got back, a place was set at the table for her. Greg pulled out her chair, and she allowed them to get their business out of the way. They had a few rounds of cocktails and some good food, and Kelley made her exit.

When they went to the valet, he asked, "So what else do you have planned for tonight?"

"Home. The kids are with my husband's parents, so I had planned an evening by the firepit with my Kindle and a glass of something."

"Oh, you have kids?" he teased.

She welcomed this fun. "Yes, twins, as a matter of fact."

"You're too sexy to have two kids."

"You think so?"

"Yes, and I'd love to have a chance to occupy some more of your time tonight," he said, and her car pulled up.

"Well, that depends."

"On?"

"If my husband comes home tonight."

"That's a bet," he said and gave her a kiss.

She went to get into her car and waited for his car to pull up. She pulled away, and he was behind her every time she glanced up at her rearview mirror. They made it back to the house and parked in their garage. She went in, stepped out of her shoes, and leaned on the counter. She wanted to make love, no doubt, but they had to have a conversation.

"What's going on, Gregory? What does this mean? I can't be a hit and quit tonight."

"This means I'm sorry too, and I want us to start over. I want to give our marriage a try."

"Do you really mean that?"

"Yes. Now go put on something comfy, and I'll try to find something around here to put on to get out of this suit, and we can talk."

She agreed, and when she finally came back, he was already out back with the pit going. He had on a pair of slides and some sweats and a hoodie from the box left in the basement that he had never picked up. "Where are the divorce papers?" he asked as soon as she stepped out the door.

"My office. Why?"

"Go and get them."

She nodded, went back inside, and returned shortly after. She handed them over to him, and he tossed them in the firepit. He pulled her in for a hug, and she just stood in his arms for as long as he held on to her. They sat, and he handed her the glass of merlot he had poured for her. They talked for hours that night, shed tears, and made vows and promises. They decided to go to counseling and do whatever it took to make their marriage work.

Chapter Thirty-nine

Janiece

That Sunday morning, she gathered her things and got ready to check out. She was confident with her decision and prayed it was right. She didn't want to hurt either of them, but she knew she would hurt one of them that day. She called to let the valet know she needed her car to be brought around. She double-checked the room to ensure she wasn't leaving anything behind and then headed to the desk.

"Mrs. Lawton, was everything okay with your stay?" the clerk asked.

"Everything was great, thanks."

"It was a pleasure to have you, and I just want to give you a reminder that you will still be charged for a full night tonight," she said with a bright smile.

"I'm aware, and that is fine."

Janiece turned, lifted the extending handle, and wheeled her luggage toward the exit. The valet opened her trunk and put her suitcase in it. A minute or two after she pulled away, her sister called.

"Hello, Janelle, and no, I'm not telling you until after I tell him."

"Hello, Janiece, and that is not why I'm calling you."

"Yeah, right. What other reason would you just so happen to be calling me for when I told you I'd be leaving the hotel?"

"Even though the suspense drives me crazy, I'm calling with good news."

"You have news today too, huh?"

"I do."

"Well, let's hear your good news, sissy."

"My husband and I are officially back together again," she sang.

"Shut up! Stop lying, Nelly," she said cheerfully. She was so happy to hear that. Greg and Janelle were a match made in heaven.

"Yes, we are. Yes, we are, chick. He is moving back in as we speak, girl," Janelle squealed.

"That is amazing, and I'm so happy for you guys."

"Thanks, and next weekend we are having people over for our last cookout of the year before this weather starts to act up. So you and whatever husband you choose will be here next Saturday."

"Ha-ha, and we will definitely be there," Janiece promised.

"And you're still not going to just tell me, Jai. You are so wrong. It's not like I will hang up and call anybody."

"Again, you will know soon enough. I'll call you later," she said and hung up.

She drove with her stomach in knots and hated that the traffic was so bad. She had given herself enough time to make it at exactly seven, but this traffic was fucking up her plans, and she knew he'd think she wasn't coming. She wanted to call, but the deal was to walk in at seven, and she didn't want to be late. When the traffic finally cleared, she put her foot on the gas and drove as fast as she could, praying no one would pull her over. She pulled into the drive and barely put the car in park before she shut off the engine and ran to the door.

When she rushed in, he was standing near the door, looking at his Rolex. "You're late."

"Traffic." She smiled.

He moved slowly in her direction. "Are you home to stay with me?" he asked and stopped in his tracks.

"Yes, I am sure. I love you and want to be here with you," she said, and her eyes quickly filled with tears.

"Come here," he said, and she walked into his arms. "I've missed you so much, woman. Promise me that you will never leave me ever again."

"I promise, K.P. I'm home for good this time. And thank you for waiting for me. This was the hardest thing I've ever had to do, but I'm glad I truly know where I want to be."

"I love you," he said and kissed her passionately. He pulled away and reached into his pocket. "I believe these belong to you," he said and slid her rings on her finger. She wrapped her arms around his neck and kissed him again. She was so happy to be back with him. She'd missed him.

They moved over to the sofa, and she asked about the kids. He told her he needed to be alone if she hadn't come home, and they'd need to be alone if she did, and she laughed. They caught up a little bit and then ended up in bed. After three months, she knew K.P. was anxious to reunite with her. After some serious making up in the sheets, they just lay and talked.

"When do you plan to talk to Isaiah?" he asked.

"Tomorrow is best. I don't want to let too much time pass before we talk about this."

"How do you feel about your decision? Because I'm never doing that shit again," he joked.

"I feel good to be here, and I know this will be hard for him, but I couldn't lie to him or myself. He deserves to be happy, and he is amazing, so he will find love again."

"I know, but a broken heart is hard to overcome."

"How do you know? Your heart hasn't been broken."

"Do I need to remind you of our last breakup, Miss I'm Not Going to Vegas?" he joked.

She tapped his arm. "Okay, why you gotta bring up ol' shit?" she laughed.

"I'm just saying. But all jokes aside, I'm proud of you for doing the right thing and making up your own mind. I am relieved that you came home to me, but at the same time, I feel for Isaiah. I know he is a good guy, and I wish him well."

"Me too. Now let me call Janelle quickly because, I swear, she has called me a thousand times."

"You do that while I go get something from the kitchen."

"Something like what?"

"You'll see. Just call your sister," he said, and she admired his ass. His body was still beautiful.

When she picked up her phone, she saw that Isaiah had called thrice. Her daughter was with him, so she called him first.

"When are you going to come for the rest of your things?" was the first thing he asked.

"I planned to come tomorrow. Is everything okay?"

"No."

"What's wrong? Is Jaiden okay?"

"Our daughter is fine, Janiece, but I'm not."

"I'll come to see you tomorrow."

"Janiece," he said, and when he called her name like that, her heart ached, and the tears formed.

"Tomorrow, I promise." She sniffled. He didn't say anything. "Isaiah?"

"I hope you are happy, and I'll see you tomorrow." He ended the call.

She called Doreen and asked if she could just go by and check on him for her. She assured her she would, and she let Janiece know that Jaiden was with them. That gave her a little relief. She couldn't imagine how he was feeling, and a part of her just wanted to get dressed and go to him, but then it would be a never-ending cycle. She gave him what he asked. They all had to live with her decision, she thought, but that didn't stop her tears.

She just texted Janelle and said, With K.P. I promise I'll call you tomorrow. When K.P. returned with champagne, glasses, and a tray of chocolate-covered strawberries, her face was drenched.

"Hey, baby, what happened just that quick?" he asked, putting the tray on the bed. He set the bubbly glass on the night table and climbed into bed with her. "Baby, what's wrong?"

"I had a few missed calls from Isaiah, so I called because something could have been wrong with Jaiden, and he sounded terrible. This is so horrible, and I feel like shit."

"Shhh, it is going to be okay. It will be okay, Jai. Today is the worst day, but it will get better."

"He sounded so bad."

"I'm sorry, honey. Maybe it's not a good time for champagne."

"But it's a good time for something harder."

"I got you. Come on," he said and got up. He went into the walk-in and came out with one of Janiece's robes, and she put it on. She headed toward the bathroom. K.P. grabbed the tray, glasses, and champagne and left the room. After she tinkled and brushed her hair into place, she went to join K.P. in the living room. He grabbed the tequila for her and the whiskey for himself. He grabbed two shot glasses and headed to the kitchen. He came back with a bowl of sliced limes and then joined her on the sofa.

"Are you planning to go into the office tomorrow?"

"Nah, I'll be working from home all week. I took this week with the idea that I'd be with my wife all week or nursing a wounded heart."

She cracked a half-smile. "Well, pour because I feel like shit. Maybe I should have just not gone back. I gave him hope, and it's like this didn't make shit any easier."

He poured and handed her the glass. "Today is just the toughest day. Trust me, it will work out."

She grabbed a lime, threw back the shot, and sucked the lime. She placed the lime on the coaster and held her glass for another. That went on for seven shots, and then there were more tears. K.P. just drank with her and just was there for her. He helped her to bed, and she thanked God as she passed out because she didn't want to cry about it anymore.

Chapter Forty

Janiece

The next day she woke up in the late afternoon and had a drum solo going on in her head. It took a moment to realize that she was back at K.P.'s and everything that had happened the day before wasn't a dream. She got up and called out his name as she went to the bathroom. As soon as she sat, he was in the doorway.

"You're finally awake," he said.

"Yes," she said, yawning and rubbing her eyes. "What time is it?"

"Almost five," he said.

"Damn, please tell me that there is coffee."

"There is, and I have some food ready for you, too."

"Thanks, baby," she said, rolling a few sheets from the tissue roll. She wiped and went over to the sink. She had dried-up saliva on the side of her face, and her mouth was dry as hell. It took her a few moments to get it together, and she was happy that her headache was subsiding on its own without a pill.

Her clothes were exactly how he had left them in her drawers and their master closet. She remembered her suitcase was in the trunk, so she asked K.P. to grab it. It had her favorite makeup items, and she decided she was still going to see Isaiah that afternoon. After she dressed, ate, and assured K.P. that he would not have to come looking for her, she headed to Isaiah's.

When she pulled into the drive, she took a few cleansing breaths and got out. She had to face this. She had to stand by her decision. She used her key to open the door and made a mental note to give it back to him. She slowly walked into an empty living room. "Hello," she called out, and then Jaiden came running into the living room.

"Mommy," she said, and Janiece picked up her little girl. She kissed her a few times, and then Isaiah walked in. He looked as good as he always did, and she took note of that and thought, *this is going to be so hard.*

"Hey," she said.

"Hey. I'm in the kitchen cooking, so you can come on in," he said and went back toward the kitchen. She looked over by the door and noticed her other two suitcases were already packed. That was no surprise. She went into the kitchen and put Jaiden down on her booster in the chair at the table. She sat, and Isaiah brought over a plate of fried chicken, mac and cheese, and broccoli and put it in front of Jaiden. "Are you hungry?" he asked.

"No, but we need to talk."

"After I put my daughter down," he said and went back over to the stove. He took a few more pieces from the pan and placed the paper towels on the counter. He turned off the fire and then sat down at the table. He didn't have food, but he had a drink. He talked a lot to the baby like all was fine, but he couldn't even look at her. When Jaiden was done with her food, he took her plate and told her to go play while he cleaned the kitchen. He turned on some music and got busy. Janiece helped herself to a glass of wine and sat at the table while he cleaned. She wondered why he was stalling, because she didn't plan to be there late.

"I'm going to give Jaiden her bath," he announced and walked off. She heard the water running after a little while. She got a refill and then decided to go up.

She set her glass down and got down on her knees to help with her bath like they always did. "Why did you start without me?"

"Because we won't be bathing her together anymore. I didn't see the point," he said.

"That's not true. We are still going to coparent, Isaiah. I'm not just going to disappear."

"I know this, Jai, damn!" he said, and she knew his behavior was just out of hurt, so she nodded.

"I'm sorry, babe, I'm so . . ." she tried to say. Her eyes burned with tears.

"Janiece, please, after we put our daughter down, okay? I don't want to do this in front of Jaiden."

"Okay," she said and stopped pushing. They did their bath routine. Same for their bed routine after lotion, pajamas, story, kisses, and lights out. "Good night, baby. Mommy loves you," she told a half-asleep Jaiden and kissed her again.

When they went downstairs, Janiece went to the family room, and Isaiah went for another drink. After him stalling for ten or fifteen minutes, he finally joined her. They were silent, but she whispered, "Isaiah, I'm sorry."

"What are you sorry about, Jai? Are you sorry for ever marrying me when you knew deep down you never got over him? Are you sorry because you wish I were dead and hadn't come back? Tell me exactly what in the hell you are sorry for, Janiece. I know I said that I'd let you go after ninety days, but you know what, Janiece? I don't want to. It's killing me, and I hate that I love you so much. I want to hate you, but I can't stop loving you," he said and let a tear fall. "I knew you would go back to him. I swear deep down inside, I knew you would go back, but I kept hoping and praying that you would find that love in your heart that you had for me before I got on that plane," he said and wiped the tears from his face.

Janiece was dying on the inside, listening to his words. "Isaiah, please, don't you think that I wish you had died for one moment. I don't want K.P. that bad to wish that you were dead. Give me some credit. I did love you so deeply at one point. Isaiah, when I married you, I felt like a wife is supposed to feel. When you left, and I thought you died, it broke me, Isaiah. It took me a long time to even let K.P. back into my heart, but he was just there and so patient and helped me to heal, and I fell in love with him all over again. I don't know why things happened this way. I can't look at you with a straight face and give you one solid answer of how, but when I thought I lost you, K.P. and Janelle were the only people I had, and your family took me through so much when I was broken. If K.P. hadn't been there, I literally would have lost my mind. I had this baby growing inside of me, and I had to tell her that her daddy died fighting for this country, and I was raw and open, and he crept back in. I thought you died," she sobbed. "I didn't just run back to him. It didn't go down like that, Isaiah. Please believe me, and I'd be a horrible person to stay here and pretend that I'm good. That is not fair to either of us. You deserve love and to be with someone who truly wants to be with you.

"I love you in so many ways. You were my husband. You are my daughter's father, but I can't force it. That fire and that passion that I had for you before, I couldn't get that back, and I know you are hurting now, but you will get over me, Isaiah, and you will fall in love again. I couldn't let guilt, pity, or all the lame reasons people stay with someone be the reason why I stayed. I owe you more than that," she said with a face full of tears. "I just couldn't do that to you, baby, so please understand and don't hate me. I love you too much to live a lie with you. You gotta believe that."

"Janiece, I could never hate you," he said, getting up. He took a seat next to her. "I know this was tough for you, and you've been through a lot, and so have I. I watched all of your diary clips and know that your decision to be with K.P. wasn't because you were glad I died, so I'll just have to take this shit one day at a time. Letting you go is going to be hard, Janiece, but at the end of the day, I want you happy and what is best for both of us. This hurts like a bitch, but I know I'll be okay in time. I asked you for ninety days, and you gave me a fair ninety days, and I don't want you to force anything or be miserable to spare my feelings. I just got to let you go," he said.

"I really hate that you got hurt, but believe me, it hurts me too. I just can't be married to you both, and God knows hurting you, and this entire situation, has been a damn battle. I just want us to finally have peace and happiness."

He pulled her into his arms. "Me too, Jai. And even though I didn't want this to end this way, this is what it is, and I will give you the divorce like I said I would. I'll call my lawyer in the morning, and we'll get the ball rolling," he said, and she looked up at him.

"Thank you, Isaiah. Thank you, and I love you for just being you. I love you for being Jaiden's father and loving me like you do. I want us to be happy families and good parents to our daughter."

"I want the same, and I love you too, Jai. I'll be okay, and we will be okay," he said and stood. He reached out to help her up. He pulled her in and held her tight. He gave her a gentle kiss on her forehead, and she let him kiss her lips. She knew that was the last kiss he'd ever put on her lips. She went up to kiss Jaiden one more time. She did a quick sweep of the upper level, and it looked as if he had packed all of her things.

He walked her out and helped put her things in the trunk. She said she'd call him the next day to check on Jaiden. She also mentioned Janelle's cookout because Janelle told her that she wanted Isaiah there, but he declined. He wasn't ready to be around K.P. just yet, and she understood that. She added that she wanted the baby to go, and he okayed it. She said good night, and he took her hand and kissed the back of it. He squeezed it tight and then said, "Goodbye, Janiece."

"Goodbye, Isaiah," she returned, and he let go and went inside.

She thought there would be no more tears, but she was wrong. She walked into K.P.'s arms and cried for Isaiah. K.P. assured her it would be okay, but she didn't believe that.

After a few days of awkwardness with Isaiah, things started to get better. Their encounters got easier, and things did get better. The guilt had faded, and she could tell that Isaiah was moving on because he seemed happier. Their conversations grew into friendly conversations, and having both K.P. and Isaiah in the same room eventually became normal and not weird.

The following spring, Jaiden was turning 2. This time, her birthday party was at Isaiah's house.

Janiece was in the kitchen preparing party plates when a woman she didn't recognize walked in. Janiece eyed the woman.

"Hello," the woman said.

"Hi," Janiece said, puzzled.

"I'm sorry. I'm Christa, a friend of Isaiah's. He told me to come on in," she said.

"Oh, hi, Christa, forgive me. I'm Janiece, Jaiden's mom. I heard about you. Come right on in," Janiece said because Isaiah mentioned seeing someone, but he didn't say how fine that someone was.

"Where can I put this?" she asked because she had a couple of pans of something covered with foil in her hands.

"There is fine," Janiece said after spotting a free spot on the counter.

"It's nice to finally meet you," she said to Janiece.

"Likewise," she replied and was happy that K.P. walked into the kitchen at that moment.

"Baby, Isaiah wants to know where the paper plates, napkins, and cups are."

"I think they are still in my trunk. Can you check?"

"I can, and hello," he said, speaking to Christa.

"Babe, this is Isaiah's friend Christa. Christa, this is my husband, K.P."

"Nice to meet you," she said.

"You too," he said and headed out the front door.

"So where did you and Isaiah meet?"

"At the gym, actually." She smiled.

At that moment, Isaiah walked in. He greeted her with a kiss, and it was more than friendly, Janiece thought, but she put her eyes back on the tray she was putting together. Christa followed Isaiah outside.

Soon after, guests started to arrive, and the party got underway. Isaiah's family came without drama, and it was a good day. After most of the small kids left, some grownups stayed behind. Janelle's kids were upstairs with Jaiden. The drinks were served, and the card table went up. They danced and had a good time.

"What did you think of Christa?" Janiece asked K.P. when they got home.

"She was cool, I guess," K.P. answered, undressing.

"She is gorgeous," she commented.

"Yeah, she's pretty," K.P. said and then looked at his wife. "Don't tell me that you are jealous," he teased, stepping into his pajama pants.

"No, no, no, I'm not jealous," she quickly protested. "I'm happy for Isaiah, you know. After all he has gone through, I wonder if she is a good fit for him, and if she is, I hope she makes him happy, that's all," she said, putting her arms around her husband's waist.

"Okay," he said and kissed her forehead.

"I love you, and thank you for being so good to me. Jaiden's party was a hit, and I know I drove you and Isaiah insane, but it had to be perfect."

"Yeah, it was a great party, and I'm glad Kimberly brought the kids. Since this was her weekend to have them, she didn't want them to miss Jaiden's party."

"I know, and speaking of the kids, I left something on the bathroom sink for you," she said and went to pull back the covers on the bed.

"What? I left the cap off the toothpaste again?" he said, walking into the bathroom.

She sat on the bench and waited for his reaction.

"Nooooo fucking way," he yelled, coming out of the bathroom with the pregnancy test stick in his hand.

"Yes fucking way, baby. We are pregnant," she screamed, getting up from the bench. He just stared at the stick.

"Baby, this is so awesome, and I am so happy," he said, pulling her into his arms. "We finally have a child together, this is so great, and I love you so much, Janiece. And I'm so happy."

"I love you too, Kerry, and I am happy for the first time in a very long time too."

The End